GERARD

BAYOU BROTHERHOOD PROTECTORS
BOOK TWO

ELLE JAMES

TWISTED PAGE INC

© 2023 Twisted Page Inc. All rights reserved.

ISBN EBOOK: 978-1-62695-518-9

ISBN PRINT: 978-1-62695-519-6

To my mother and father. Not a day goes by that I don't think about you and miss you. You gave me the best childhood. Wish I could hug you once more. I love you so much!

Elle James

AUTHOR'S NOTE

Enjoy other protector books by Elle James

Bayou Brotherhood Protectors
Remy (#1)
Gerard (#2)
Lucas (#3)
Beau (#4)
Rafael (#5)
Valentin (#6)
Landry (#7)
Simon (#8)
Maurice (#9)
Jacques (#10)

Visit ellejames.com for more titles and release dates
Join her newsletter at
https://ellejames.com/contact/

GERARD

BAYOU BROTHERHOOD PROTECTORS
BOOK #2

New York Times & *USA Today*
Bestselling Author

ELLE JAMES

PROLOGUE

THERE THEY WERE AGAIN.

Headlights in his rearview mirror nearly blinded him.

Was it them? Had they caught up with him?

His heart hammered against his ribs as he rammed his foot onto the accelerator, wishing he had stolen a faster car. One with more gas in the tank and an air conditioner that worked. Instead, he had taken an older model boat of a car that hadn't been locked and was easy to hotwire. He'd ridden with the windows down to catch a breeze in the stifling southern Louisiana humidity.

He'd left New Orleans a little over an hour ago with his tail in hot pursuit.

And why wouldn't they be?

He glanced at the ordinary gym bag sitting on the

3

seat beside him and shivered. What the hell was he doing? Were the contents of that bag worth his life?

Taking it had been too easy.

Keeping it...not so much.

As soon as he'd grabbed the bag and run, they'd been after him. He'd lost them a couple of times in the streets of New Orleans and on the backroads west of the city. Each time, they'd caught up to him.

The bag had to be tagged with some kind of tracking device. If he could get a free minute, he'd stop, find the device and toss it. Trouble was, he hadn't had a free moment, the gas gauge had been sitting on E for the past thirty miles and he had run out of options.

When he'd seen the sign for Bayou Mambaloa, he'd turned off the main highway onto the parish road.

He remembered his father talking about his boyhood home. The home he hadn't returned to in over thirty-odd years.

When the Mambaloa Boat Factory had closed, the community had practically dried up. Fewer jobs had meant no future for young people. His father had left when he was in his twenties never looked back. His one regret had been leaving his high school sweetheart behind.

The key feature of Bayou Mambaloa that interested him now was that it was a town so small it barely warranted a dot on a map. Sitting on the edge of a bayou, he could steal a boat and lose the bastards behind him.

If they didn't catch up to him before he reached the bayou.

If he could get to the bayou before he ran out of gas.

The trailing vehicle closed in on him. A loud bang sounded, his rear window exploded and a sharp pain knifed through his left shoulder, rendering his left arm useless.

With only his right hand on the wheel, he took a curve without slowing, sending the car's tail spinning out behind him. The rear tires regained traction and shot him forward. For a few precious seconds, the low-hanging trees blocked the headlights, which meant they couldn't see him either. A narrow dirt track ahead might be his only chance to lose the vehicle behind him.

Gunning the accelerator, he raced for the dirt track and spun the steering wheel to the right, sending the tank of a car down the rutted path. He prayed the track would take him deeper into the woods where his pursuers wouldn't find him and maybe close to a marina where he could find a boat and speed away into the bayou. He killed the head-lights even as he mashed his foot on the accelerator, slamming through the brush and mowing over small trees and bushes.

God, he hoped there wasn't a tree in front of him. His night vision had yet to adjust to the lack of head-lights. About the time he could make out more than the ruts in the dirt track, he emerged in a small clear-ing, with brush on either side and a dark maw ahead, sloping downward. He didn't dare hit the brakes and shine the red taillights, giving away his position. The car's forward momentum carried him through the clearing and down the slope.

A break in the overhead foliage let starlight through, the light reflecting off a smooth, glassy surface.

Too late.

He plowed into the water, the front end of the vehicle nosediving into the swamp. The impact jerked him forward, slamming his forehead against the steering wheel.

For a second, darkness enveloped him.

He blinked several times, forcing back a wave of dizziness. When he could see out the front wind-shield, he stared at the bayou.

Fortunately, the water wasn't deep enough to submerge the car. The front tires sank into the silt, sending the engine under while the back wheels remained on the bank.

His left arm hung loose, and warm blood soaked

his shirt, making it stick to the skin on his chest. He'd been hit. Bad. If he didn't get out of the swamp and find a hospital, the guys who'd been following him would be the least of his worries.

As his strength weakened, he shifted into reverse and hit the accelerator.

The engine coughed once and died, waterlogged, steam whooshing from beneath the hood.

He tried to push the door open with his injured shoulder and winced. The door wouldn't budge. After dragging the gym bag across the console, he turned in his seat with his back to the door. With his good hand, he pulled himself out of the driver's seat and sat in the window frame.

For a second, he hesitated, the stars overhead blurring.

His father had told him of the alligators that lived in the bayou. Some grew as long as seventeen feet and weighed over five hundred pounds. And they were most active at night.

With no other choice, he swung his legs out of the car and dropped down into the water, sinking six inches into silt. When he tried to move his feet, the suction made it difficult.

A light shone through the foliage, bouncing toward him. Men's voices murmured in thick air.

Leaning into the car, he grabbed the bag from the console and waded to the shore. If he didn't get moving faster, the alligators would be the least of his worries.

Once he made it up the bank, he pushed through the brush, following the shoreline, trying to move silently but not succeeding. Leaves crinkled, branches snapped, and the damned frogs and cicadas had decided to shut the fuck up. It was as if they wanted him to be found by the men tracking him.

A spotlight from a boat shone across the water, aiming toward the shoreline.

He ducked low as the light swept over his position, continuing toward the men following him. It stopped, shining brightly at something.

A voice sounded over a bullhorn, "Parish Sheriff's Department. Raise your hands above your head!"

A shot rang out, the spotlight waivered and a boat motor revved, moving the boat quickly toward the shoreline.

"Put down your weapons and raise your hands in the air," the voice blared over the bullhorn.

Another shot rang out.

The boat swerved and then righted. Return fire popped off from the boat.

Swear words and footsteps crunching through the underbrush moved away from where he hunkered low in the brush.

The boat ran up on the shore, and the men on board jumped out and gave chase.

With his pursuers being pursued, he gathered what little strength he had and headed in the opposite direction.

After several hundred yards, he doubled back in the direction he hoped he'd find the road. After fighting his way through thick brush and thorny vines, he broke out of the woods and ran into a barbed-wire fence, the sharp prongs slicing into his legs and torso before he realized a fence was there. Beyond the fence stretched a long field with plants lying close to the ground with rounded humps scattered throughout. Light shone from the corner of a barn on the far side of the field. If he could make it to the barn, he might find a house nearby and another vehicle.

With his good hand, he grabbed a fencepost, planted his foot on the middle strand of the barbed wire and swung his leg over the top, planting it on the same wire on the other side. He was swinging his other leg over when a shout sounded.

"Putain de merde!" a voice said from nearby.

Two shadowy figures rose from the plants in the field. One held a large object shaped like a watermelon in his hands.

Fear spiked, and he flung himself away from the fence. The hem of his jeans caught on a barb, and he tumbled to the ground, wrenching his shoulder. Pain knifed through him, and his head swam. He could barely move; his clothes were soaked from his blood, and he wasn't sure he could get up again. Even the stars overhead blinked in and out. Dark. Bright. Dark.

Must get up. Keep moving.

So tired.

Hurt.

His thoughts, like his vision, faded in and out, confused, unfocused.

How had the men who'd been following him gotten away from the police and ahead of him into the field?

The stars blinked brightly again.

His strength waning, he dragged himself to his feet, shifted the bag barely hanging on his good shoulder and staggered away from the men in the field. He prayed they couldn't get a bead on him. If they did, he hoped they made it a clean shot, ending his life quickly.

With his gaze pinned to the light shining on the corner of the barn, he moved one foot after the other. Each step was harder than the last as he waded through thick vines, trying to avoid tripping over fat watermelons all around him.

Halfway to the barn, his knees buckled. He fell forward, his face slamming into a fat, ripe melon, cracking it open. His face slipped into the wet flesh of the melon, the sweet juice touching his lips.

He tried to push himself up from the ground, but his good arm wouldn't move. He'd lost too much blood. The thumping pulse in his ears steadily slowed.

"Dude," a male voice, thick with a Cajun accent, sounded close. "Do he be dead?"

"Don't know," a guy with a deeper voice said.

Not dead, he thought. *Yet.* Unable to move, he tried to force air past his vocal cords.

A booted foot pushed into his hip.

"What's he got in da bag?" Cajun Man leaned down, pulled the bag from his shoulder and unzipped it. "*Fils de pute!* Is dat what I tink dat is?"

"Gimme that," the man with the deep voice said. A second later, he whistled softly. "That's a shit-ton of money in there." His feet moved. "Holy, fuckin' shit. Git down." The men dropped to the ground.

"Dude. You dead?" A hand touched his injured shoulder and jerked back. "*Merde!* He's covered in blood."

"Whoever shot this motherfucker will be lookin' for him," deep voice man said, "and this bag of money."

"Tink it be counterfeit?" Cajun Man asked softly.

"Not if it's worth killin' fer. It's gotta be the real deal. Come on. Let's get outta here."

"What about da melons?" Cajun Man said.

"Fuck the melons." Deep Voice man zipped the

11

bag. "Don't need no stinkin' melons when we got a sack o' cash."

"But we promised Ol' Man Beaufoy we'd bring him da melons for tomorrow's farmer's market."

"I don't give a fuck about the old man's melons. We need to get rid of this body so whoever' lookin' fer him don't look 'round these parts."

"De man's not a goner yet," Cajun Man said.

No. I'm alive. But for how much longer?

"Help me drag him to the bayou." A meaty hand gripped his injured arm.

Pain ripped through him, and he blacked out.

When he came to, he was being dragged across the vines and watermelons. A smell so intense it nearly choked him filled his nostrils.

"What if da 'gators don't clean him up?" Cajun Man asked. "Da remains will come to da surface."

The two men stopped and dropped him to the ground.

The haze of semi-consciousness ebbed and flowed over him as the two men discussed how to get rid of his body.

"We could weigh him down." Deep Voice coughed. "God damn pigs."

"*Putein!*" Cajun man swore. "Dem hogs smell like death."

"No fuckin' kiddin'," said Deep Voice. "We gotta

get rid of him so those lookin' fer him'll never find him."

"Yesiree," the other man said. "Dat way we keep da cash with no one da wiser."

He didn't have the energy to tell them that the men he'd taken the bag of cash from would stop at nothing to get the money back.

"Need a way to dispose of him so's nobody finds any part of him," Deep Voice said.

A loud grunting sounded close by.

"It'll take dern near forever ta get 'im to da bayou. I vote fer tossin' him in da pigpen. Dey'll clean him up, bones 'n all."

Fat raindrops plopped onto the back of his head and neck.

"Better hurry before it starts rainin' pitchforks and hammer handles," Cajun Man said.

A loud honking sounded.

"What the hell?" Deep Voice cried out.

More honking and flapping wings whipped up the air around them as rain began to fall in earnest.

"Get this goddamn bird off me," Deep Voice yelled.

"Tryin'," Cajun grunted. "Biggest damned goose ever I saw."

The goose's honk was cut off in a distressed squeak.

Deep Voice grunted. "Die, motherfucker."

"You done broke her neck," Cajun Man said. "She be one dead goose."

The bird dropped beside him and lay still, the feathers brushing softly against his arm.

"Can't leave it by the pigpen. It'll draw attention to the hogs 'fore they've had a chance ta do their work," Deep Voice said.

"Should carry it on back to da farmhouse," Cajun Man said. "Maybe she won't look farther afield."

"I'll let you do that. We been here long enough," Deep Voice said, "and makin' enough noise to wake the dead."

"Iffn' we don't leave outta here soon," Cajun Man said, "Bernie'll be up and loadin' our backsides wit' buckshot."

"Check fer a pulse," Deep Voice said. "Don't want no part of murder."

"Da goose or da dude?"

"Jesus fuckin' Christ," Deep Voice growled. "Get the fuck outta my way."

As someone pressed thick fingers to the base of his throat, the stars blinked out one last time.

"Dead as a doornail," Deep Voice said. "Don'tcha know that whoever shot this guy will be looking for that bag."

"Not just worried 'bout da shooters," Cajun Man said. "Da Popo might decide to come dis way lookin' fer the dead guy and the bag."

"Fuck," Deep Voice said. "Help me strip him and get him into the pigpen."

As he faded into death, his last thought was of the irony of his life and death. He'd loved bacon, sometimes consuming a complete package at a time for breakfast. How fitting he'd be consumed by a hog that would someday end up as bacon on someone else's breakfast table.

CHAPTER 1

GERARD GUIDRY ORDERED A BEER, burger and fries at the Crawdad Hole Bar and Grill and settled back, ready to relax and celebrate the grand opening of the Bayou Brotherhood Protectors.

Once the waitress returned with a round of mugs full of foaming beer, the men of his new team all lifted their glasses.

"To new beginnings," Landry Laurent said.

Sinclaire "Sin" Sevier held up a hand. "No, no, no. What the hell kind of toast is that? We need something stronger, more masculine—"

"And kickass?" Their waitress, Danielle French, propped her tray on one hip and her fist on the other. "How about, *To inflated egos, muscle-bound, spitting, farting and beer-drinking men who've taken Bayou Mambaloa by storm?*"

Gerard laughed. "That's closer to the truth."

"No, it needs to be something grand and memorable," Sin said.

"What Danni said was memorable." Lucas LeBlanc lifted his mug. "Here! Here!"

The others joined him, shouting at the tops of their lungs.

Sin's lips curled in disdain. "I'm in with a bunch of ingrates who wouldn't know pomp and circumstance if it bit them in the butt."

"We can't toast anyway until Remy gets here," Beau Boyette noted. "He's our leader. He needs to be the one to bless this motley crew."

The others nodded and drank their beer.

Rafael "Romeo" Romero set his mug on the table and wiped the foam from his mouth. "So, who do you think will get the first assignment?"

"Remy and Gerard had the first assignment before the rest of us got here," Valentin Vachon reminded them.

"True," Beau said. "Now that the building is cleaned out and we're all settled in either the boarding house or other accommodations, we need to work to earn the pay we're getting from Hank Patterson at our higher headquarters in Montana."

"It's only a matter of time," Gerard said. "Hank's got connections. I'm sure he was waiting for us to settle things here before he opened the floodgates."

Romeo clapped his hands together and rubbed them eagerly. "I hope I'm assigned to guard a rich heiress. Be nice to live the high life after digging foxholes in the sandbox."

Jacques Jardine snorted. "Won't that put a crimp in your efforts to woo the pretty gift shop owner?"

"I'm not wooing anyone," Romeo said.

"You spend a lot of time in that gift shop," Jacques said.

Romeo frowned. "She has interesting things to look at."

Jacques laughed. "I'll bet."

"I'm not wooing her," Romeo insisted.

Xavier Xander leaned forward, his eyebrows arching. "Then you won't mind if I go after the gorgeous Gisele?"

Romeo's eyes narrowed, and his lips pressed into a straight line. Finally, he shrugged. "She has a mind of her own."

"Fair game," Xavier said with a grin.

"I'd go for protecting a rich tycoon on his yacht in the Mediterranean." Valentin brought them back to their wish lists. "Been a while since I've been on a marine mission."

"I wouldn't mind being a bodyguard to a wealthy financial advisor," Beau said. "I could use some good tips to increase the value of my investment portfolio."

Gerard lifted his beer. "I'll take anything I can get.

I don't like sitting around twiddling my thumbs." As he lifted his mug to his lips, his cell phone vibrated on the table in front of him.

Romeo leaned over and grinned. "It's Remy. Maybe he's got something for you…?"

Gerard lifted the cell phone and received the call.

Before he could say hello, Remy jumped in with, "Gerard, I have an assignment for you."

Gerard glanced up at the men all staring at him. "Great. I'm ready. What do I have to do?" His mind sped ahead of Remy with thoughts of guarding an heiress, a politician or a celebrity.

"I need you to find out who killed Bernie Bellamy's goose."

Gerard frowned. "I'm sorry. Did you say…" he covered his mouth and whispered into the phone, "goose?"

"I did," Remy said.

"Uh. Okay. I guess," Gerard said, not exactly sure how he could be of assistance, never having been around farm animals. "When do I start?"

"No time like the present," Remy said.

"Gotcha." Gerard sat in stunned silence as Remy gave him the address of Bellamy Acres.

"Your client is Bernie Bellamy. Good luck. I know you'll do the Bayou Brotherhood proud."

"Yes, sir." Gerard ended the call and pushed back from the table.

"Did you get your first assignment?" Beau asked.

Gerard nodded and slipped his cell phone in his pocket. "I'm to investigate a murder."

Romeo grinned. "I swear I heard you say goose. Is your first solo client a goose?"

Gerard frowned. "Yes, and no. My client is a Bernie Bellamy. I'm to investigate the murder of her goose."

The men at the table burst out laughing.

"Oh, this is going to be rich." Sin rubbed his hands together. "Do we get to come along and watch the master sleuth at work as he discovers the identity of the killer?"

Gerard shook his head. "No way. Stay and drink your beer."

"You look worried," Romeo said. "Afraid you'll be chasing a wild goose?" He chuckled. "No, wait. The goose is dead. Not much chasing there."

Gerard ignored the hecklers and left the Crawdad Hole, climbed onto his motorcycle and keyed in the address of Bellamy Acres.

The directions sent him driving through the small town of Bayou Mambaloa and southeast along the edge of the bayou. Eventually, he came to the turn off the highway and stopped at a gate with an arched sign with the words BELLAMY ACRES carved out of sheet metal.

He rolled across the cattle guard and followed the

gravel road to a white, two-story farmhouse with a wraparound porch. A large, spotted hound dog lifted his head, assessed Gerard and laid back down to sleep.

Two trucks were parked in front of the house. One was a one-ton, white work truck with mud splattered up to its axles. The other was a vintage truck with shiny green paint and black wheel fenders. The rear of the old truck had been retrofitted with handy produce bins and shelves labeled for jellies, preserves, pickles and honey. BELLAMY ACRES had been stenciled across the doors of the vintage truck, but the produce bins and marked shelves were empty.

A tall, slender woman stepped out of the house onto the front porch, shading her eyes with her hand. "Can I help you?" she asked.

"I'm looking for Mr. Bellamy," Gerard said.

She stiffened. "He's not here."

Undaunted, Gerard walked to the base of the porch steps. "Remy Montagne sent me to talk to him. Could you tell me where I can find him?"

Her eyes narrowed. "Head back the way you came and turn at the Bayou Mambaloa Cemetery Road. You'll find him there."

"Thank you, ma'am," Gerard started to turn.

"Wait." The woman descended the steps. "He's there, but you won't be talking to him."

"Why?" Gerard asked. "Is he busy?"

She shook her head. "No. He's dead."

Gerard frowned. "I don't understand. Remy said I was to come to Bellamy Acres and ask for Bernie Bellamy."

Her lips twitched.

Gerard sighed. "Let me guess...you're Bernie Bellamy."

She nodded and held out her hand. "Bernadette Bellamy. I go by Bernie."

Gerard shook her hand and gave her a twisted grin. "Gerard Guidry. Pleasure to meet you." His frown returned. "My apologies if my asking for Mr. Bellamy was upsetting. My condolences. How long has your father been gone?"

"Not my father. My husband." She stared down at their joined hands. "He's been gone three years."

Gerard quickly released his grip on her long, slender fingers. "I'm sorry... I assumed... Hell. You look too young to be a widow."

A shadow crossed over her gray eyes. Bernie shrugged. "We don't always get a choice of when we die." She walked past him to her work truck. "If Remy sent you, I assume it's to help me figure out who killed Gertrude." She leaned over the tailgate and nodded to the contents contained in the bed. "I found her this morning on my front porch. Her neck had been broken."

Gerard stared at the white goose covered in mud. "Any footprints leading up to the porch?"

Bernie shook her head, her long blond ponytail swinging softly behind her. The woman wasn't exactly beautiful, but she wasn't hard to look at. Taller than most women, she could look him in the eye without having to tilt her head back too much. She had a wholesome, girl-next-door appeal some men would find attractive.

Not Gerard. He went for seasoned women who didn't expect commitment.

She walked back to stand below the porch. "I found Gertie here." She patted the porch while inspecting the ground below. "It was raining so hard last night that any footprints would've been washed away."

"Were any other animals harmed?" he asked. "Any missing?"

"I checked all the animals around the barn and at the stock pond where Gertrude normally spends the night. Gandolf was there, floating around like nothing was amiss."

"Gandolf?"

"Gertrude's mate." She glanced over his shoulder at the road leading into the farm. "I can show you where she usually stayed. I've walked all around the pond and found no feathers indicating a struggle."

"I'd like to check it out," Gerard said.

Bernie nodded and tipped her chin toward the road. "I'm expecting a truckload of farm workers soon to help pick watermelons and other produce. We can look around until they arrive, then I'll have to cut loose to help with the harvest. Anything you can do to find out who might've been on the farm last night will help."

Gerard followed Bernie to the barn, wondering how a Marine Force Recon operative who'd never been around animals other than observing Military Working Dogs from a distance could help find a goose killer. This being his first solo assignment with Bayou Brotherhood Protectors, he couldn't fail the team. No matter how ridiculous the task seemed.

Bernie waved toward the pond, where a lone white goose floated across the surface, seemingly unfazed by his missing mate. "My geese are good at guarding the property. It could be that she attacked an intruder, whether it was four-legged or two-legged, and got killed for her effort. I need to know what happened so I can protect the other animals. Plus, I need to know why who or whatever killed it left it on my porch—for my peace of mind."

Gerard held up his hands. "I'll do what I can, but I've never investigated the murder of a farm animal."

She gave him a crooked smile. "Sometimes, a fresh set of eyes helps. Maybe just your presence will keep the intruder from striking again and give us time to identify him."

She was willing to give the city boy a chance. The least he could do was give it his best effort, starting with learning more about his client and her life at Bellamy Acres. "Have you always been a farmer?" Gerard asked.

Bernie stopped in front of a wooden fence and leaned on the top rail, staring out at the odd collection of animals. "This small farm has been in my husband's family for over two hundred years. It once was over two hundred acres. Over the years, prior generations sold off portions until now it's only fifty acres. When I married Ray, I didn't have any experience farming or raising animals. But I learned. We worked the farm together until he couldn't work the farm anymore, and then he died. He was the last of his family line."

"No children?" Gerard studied her, imagining she'd make a good mother as much as she cared about the animals on her place.

Bernie shook her head. "No."

"What happened to your husband?" Gerard asked, curious about this relatively young woman who was the sole owner of a working farm, managing its operation single-handedly.

Bernie stared out at the animals. "He was thirty-one when he got sick. It took the doctors several months to diagnose his condition. When they did, they gave him two to five years to live."

"Cancer?" Gerard guessed.

She snorted. "If only. So many cancers can be beaten or at least pushed into remission. No, Ray was diagnosed with Amyotrophic Lateral Sclerosis, also known as Lou Gehrig's disease."

Gerard's chest tightened. "ALS." As far as he knew, there was no cure for the disease. "I'm sorry."

She sighed. "He didn't last two and a half years. Between taking care of him and the farm, the farm took a backseat. The fields went fallow. I only grew enough produce for our own use and took care of the animals the best I could. After he passed, it took me three years to bring the farm production back to where we had it before his diagnosis."

"You did that all on your own?" Gerard shook his head, impressed at her strength and determination. "Did you ever stop to breathe?"

She shook her head. "No. I focused on the future. It kept me from thinking too much about the past."

"Ever thought about selling the farm?" he asked. "I can imagine this place is a lot of work. Especially for one person."

"I've had offers. Recent offers." She frowned. "A company out of Florida has been buying land all around the farm. They want to put in a golf resort and need my place because it's good, solid ground they could build the actual resort buildings on. Bellamy Acres is smack-dab in the middle of the other tracts. It's the only thing holding them up from moving forward on construction."

"You said no," Gerard said.

"What else could I say?" She nodded toward the animals in the field beyond. "This farm was my husband's. The animals are the children we never had. We'd held off on a family until we got the farm producing. Then Ray got the diagnosis. He said it would be careless and heartless to have children when he carried the gene for ALS. He didn't wish the condition on anyone, especially any children we might have had." Her words caught.

Gerard understood Bernie's husband's desire not to pass on bad traits to his children all too well. He'd avoided marriage and children for that very reason.

Bernie squared her shoulders. "I didn't bring you here to feel sorry for me or Bellamy Acres. I asked for help to protect my little family of critters. It's too late for Gertrude, but I hope it isn't too late for the others." She gave him a watery smile. "Let me introduce you to my family."

"Uh. Okay." Gerard could see the animals meant a lot to Bernie. Though he had no experience with pets, big or small, he followed her through the gate and into the field.

The herd of creatures all came running at once.

Though the stampede intimidated the hell out of Gerard, he stepped in front of Bernie to protect her from being overrun. Then he cringed, braced himself and prepared to be trampled to death.

Bernie chuckled and placed a gentle hand on his arm. "It's okay. They won't hurt us."

"Are you sure about that?" Even as he asked the question, the animals came to an abrupt halt in front of them.

Bernie stepped around Gerard, reaching out to run her hand along the neck of a light brownish-red llama. "This is Lucy, the llama. She's a little goofy, but loveable. And here comes Desi."

The bold, black and white llama strutted up to Bernie, his head held high.

"Desi is flamboyant and cocky," Bernie said. "Aren't you, big boy?" she crooned. "I caution all men to avoid looking him in the eye."

Gerard frowned. "Why?"

"He takes it as a challenge to his dominance."

"Will he attack?" Gerard looked at Bernie, keeping Desi firmly in his peripheral vision.

"Sort of." Bernie's lips quirked. "He spits." She patted the llama's neck and fished a carrot out of her pocket. After she broke it in half, she gave one piece to Lucy and the other to Desi. They trotted off to chew their treats, making room for the other animals that were not quite as tall or intimidating.

A soft gray donkey, not much bigger than the hound dog Gerard had seen sleeping on the front porch of the house, nuzzled Bernie's hand.

She smoothed her fingers over the donkey's nose and scratched behind its ear. "This is Dom DeLuise, the miniature donkey who thinks he's a dog."

"A dog?" Gerard's eyes narrowed. "How so?"

"Watch." Bernie held up a carrot. "Sit."

Dom DeLuise dropped down on his ass.

"Roll over," Bernie commanded.

The donkey rolled over and jumped up, his tail swishing.

"Good, Dom," she cooed and gave him the treat.

Dom DeLuise trotted off to munch his carrot.

Gerard shook his head.

"He grew up with Howey Mandell, the hound dog you might've seen on the porch when you drove up," Bernie smiled. "I tried to train Howey to sit and roll over. He wasn't very receptive, but Dom picked up quickly and likes dog treats as much as carrots."

With the donkey out of the way, several goats moved closer, bleating for their turn and pushing their noses into Bernie's hand.

"The brown and white Boer goat is Elvis. Don't turn your back on him. He has a bad habit of sneaking up behind you and butting you when you least expect him."

She gave Elvis a piece of a carrot and shooed

him away. "The black Spanish goat is Maleficent. The three smaller goats are her triplets, Flora, Fauna & Merryweather. Sometimes, I take the donkey and the female goats to local events and set up a petting zoo. It's a good way for children to get familiar with farm animals and for the animals to earn their keep."

Bernie pointed to the other end of the pasture where a brown and white cow lazily munched on grass. "That's Dolly, our milk cow. I milk her morning and evening and sell her milk at the store in town. I also make butter to sell at the farmer's market."

"Where do you find time to do all this?" Gerard asked.

Bernie shrugged. "What else would I do with my time?"

"Go out to dinner with friends. Go dancing. Travel," he suggested.

She laughed. "My friends are all married with families of their own. I never learned to dance, and travel is out of the question." She raised her hands, palms upward. "Who would take care of the animals while I was gone? They need me. And frankly, I need to be needed."

"What did you do before you married Ray and his farm?"

Bernie smiled softly.

Again, he thought, not beautiful, but pretty in a way that made him want to hug her.

"I took care of my grandparents," she answered, her tone matter-of-fact.

"What do you mean?"

"My parents died in a head-on collision with a drunk driver when I was in high school. My grand-parents took me in. They were older, having had my mother when they were in their forties. By the time I graduated high school, their health was failing. I worked part-time at the feed store and took care of my grandparents."

"College?" Gerard asked.

She smiled as she walked around the banks of the small pond. "I did it all online, graduating with a degree in business with an emphasis on marketing." She looked around at the animals. "I do some online consulting for a little extra money for feed and seed."

"In your spare time," Gerard murmured. Which had to be nonexistent. He was tired just thinking about everything this woman accomplished in a twenty-four-hour day.

Bernie led the way out of the pasture, closing the gate behind them.

Gerard followed her to a small structure surrounded by tightly woven chicken wire.

She bent to turn the handle on a faucet that hung over the small trough inside the chicken run. Water ran out of the spigot into the small trough. When it was full, Bernie turned it off and straightened. "I let the chickens out during the day to range feed and put them up at night to keep them from being eaten by raccoons, coyotes or stray dogs." She looked around as if searching for something.

"Where is he?" she murmured.

"Where's who?"

"Rhett Butler, my Rhode Island Red rooster." She walked around the coop and returned to stand near Gerard. "He's a sneaky bastard. If he's around when I'm collecting eggs," she pointed to a fish net hanging on the outside of the coop, "I scoop him up in the net, hang him on the wall and go about my business. When I'm done, I release him."

"Why do you hang him on the wall?" Gerard asked. This farming business was beyond strange.

"He's got really sharp spurs," Bernie said. "He likes to nail you from behind when you're squatting down to collect eggs." She frowned. "Trust me. I have scars."

Gerard found himself curious about this woman's scars. His groin tightened.

"Come on." Bernie tipped her head to the side. "I'll show you the barn, and then we'll go out to the pigpen. I need to feed them and give them fresh water."

She opened the big door on the front of the barn, stepped in and flipped a switch.

Lights blinked on overhead, illuminating the interior of the large barn. Hay was stacked in one corner. Several stalls lined each side, and there was a room with a door.

"This is the tack room. I have saddles, bridles and leads. We used to have horses, but I don't have much time to ride."

"Understandable."

"I sold the horses after Ray died." She pointed to a four-wheeler parked in one of the open stalls. "I use the ATV when I need to get around when it's too muddy for the truck, like now. I keep hay and feed in here as well as my store of seeds I use to plant my produce."

A three-legged cat limped out of the shadows and rubbed against Bernie's leg.

"This is Eileen." Bernie grinned. "Get it?"

Gerard looked at the cat. "Did you name her after a famous actress?"

Bernie sighed. "Not many people pick up on her name."

Gerard thought harder.

Meanwhile, Bernie slung her leg over the seat of the ATV, twisted the key and pressed the start button. The engine chugged for a moment, then engaged, roaring to life.

His focus on the three-legged cat named Eileen, Gerard walked slowly toward Bernie.

When it hit him, he laughed out loud. "I get it. Not E. I. L. E. E. N. You mean it to be 'I lean.'"

Bernie grinned. "She came to me as a kitten. I don't know how she was hurt, but she was dragging one injured leg. It was badly infected, and the bone was crushed. To save the kitten, the vet amputated her leg." Bernie leaned over to scratch the cat's chin. "She's the best mouser we've ever had." She tipped her head over her shoulder. "Hop on."

Gerard swung his leg over the seat and settled behind her.

"Hold on," she said and gave the ATV some gas.

The vehicle shot forward, almost unseating Gerard.

He flung his arms around Bernie's waist and held on as she drove the four-wheeler out of the barn and into a field on the opposite side of the barn from the pasture. She slowed as she passed long rows of green, growing things.

"That's my produce garden. I grow four kinds of squash, three kinds of lettuce, mustard greens, okra, corn, purple-hull peas, onions, tomatoes, asparagus, rhubarb, strawberries, blueberries and figs."

She nodded toward the field ahead. "The big field is full of watermelon, cantaloupe and honeydew melons." She slowed. "What the hell?"

Gerard leaned around her. "What?"

"How did she get out?" She stood on the footrests.

"No, no, no!" Bernie dropped down, gunned the throttle and raced along the side of the field, stopping when she came even with a large hulk of an animal, standing in the middle of the field of watermelons.

Bernie leaped off the ATV and ran toward the animal that had to weigh ten times as much as the woman.

Gerard ran after her, leaping over vines crowded with large, fat watermelons. Some of the melons were broken open, the vines uprooted.

"Penelope Pitstop!" Bernie yelled. "Back to the pen." She waved her hands at the pig, circling her and then urging her toward a pen on the far side of the watermelon patch.

The huge pig moved slowly, rooting her nose through the vines and stopping to break open yet another melon to gobble up the juicy insides.

"No, no, no." Bernie slapped the animal's hindquarters. "Go to the pen, you greedy pig."

Penelope grunted, finished the melon and moved on.

Four melons later, she reached the pigpen and grunted a greeting to the other animals contained inside.

Bernie unhooked a heavy chain and opened the gate wide. The pig trotted through, happily joining her swine family while Bernie closed and secured the gate with the chain. "I don't understand," she said as she walked around the pen, inspecting the thick bull panels. "How did she get out? The gate was closed, the chain in place. There aren't any holes or trenches beneath the wire."

Gerard followed her, looking for any signs of damage to the enclosure but finding none. The smell was overwhelming. When they'd completed a full circuit around the pen, they stopped at the gate.

"It was closed." Bernie shook her head and turned to stare at the field of melons and clapped a hand to her forehead. "She must have been out all night." She waved her hand at the destruction. "She's decimated half the crop."

Gerard looked from the field back to the pen. "Could someone have let her out?"

"How else could she have gotten loose and the gate be closed with the chain in place when we got here? There are no holes in the pen. Ray built it to withstand an elephant."

Gerard peered through the wire into the pen at the quagmire of mud the pigs seemed content to wallow in, chewing on whatever they'd found to eat.

Something pale and white stuck out of the mud near one of the fence panels.

Penelope the pig nudged it with her snout.

"Wait," Gerard said. "What's that she's sniffing?" He dropped to a squat, reached through one of the rectangular gaps in the wire and grabbed the object before Penelope could snatch it into her greedy mouth.

He straightened with it in his hand, rubbing away the mud. "This looks like a..." His hand froze as recognition struck like a punch to the gut. "It's a foot."

"A what?" Bernie leaned close. "Holy shit. That's a human foot."

CHAPTER 2

BERNIE STAGGERED BACKWARD. "Where did you get that?"

"From inside the pigpen," Gerard said.

"How..." Bernie shook her head. "How did it get there?"

"Probably the same way Penelope got out." Gerard stared from the foot to the pen. "I believe this pigpen just became a crime scene." He laid the foot on the ground, scrubbed his hands down his jeans and then pulled his cell phone from his pocket.

Bernie couldn't quite wrap her mind around what she was looking at. "A foot in my pigpen." She glanced up. "Where's the owner of the foot?" Her gaze went to the pen, her eyes rounding. "You don't think..."

Gerard punched 911 and waited. "This is Gerard

Guidry. I'm with Bernie Bellamy at Bellamy Acres. We've discovered a human foot inside her pigpen. No. Just the foot. We haven't gone into the pen, so we don't know what else might be in there. Yes, ma'am. We'll be here. We'll wait. Thank you." He ended the call. "Sheriff's on the way." He lifted his cell phone a second time and scrolled through his contacts, selecting one.

Bernie wrapped her arms around herself, a chill slithering down her spine despite the hot, humid air of the Louisiana afternoon. "Who are you calling now?"

"Remy," Gerard said into the phone. "We have a situation here at Bellamy Acres. You might want to be here when the sheriff arrives." He explained what they'd found, his gaze on the foot lying against the ground. "It's big enough, it probably belonged to a man. No, we haven't seen any other parts... Okay...see you in a minute." He ended the call and met Bernie's gaze.

"What the hell?" Bernie said. "First, Gertrude. Now this?" She shook her head, her body trembling.

Gerard's brow dipped. "Hey." He reached out and pulled her into his arms. "Are you okay?"

"No. I'm not okay. You realize pigs eat everything." She waved a hand out behind her. "I mean, look at what Penelope did in a few short hours. There are a lot of swine in that pen. If they've been working on whatever was thrown in there since last night's storm, there might not be anything left to find."

Gerard's arms tightened around her. "The sheriff will have someone sift through the mud. If there's anything left to find, they'll collect it and send it to the state crime lab. The foot alone will provide a DNA sample."

Bernie leaned her forehead against Gerard's chest, thankful for his strength and the arms wrapped around her. It had been so long since anyone had held her close.

A twinge of guilt rippled through her. The last man to hold her had been her husband as he lay on his deathbed.

Was it wrong of her to like how Gerard's arms felt around her? Was she being disloyal to her dead husband's memory?

Sirens sounded in the distance.

Bernie straightened, moving away from Gerard and his warm, strong arms. A shiver rippled through her body as she moved away from his heat. "I'd better head for the house to meet the authorities. You might want to stay here and guard that...thing...to keep animals from taking off with it."

Gerard nodded. "Are you going to be all right?"

She gave him a weak smile. "I don't have a choice. The foot appeared on my property. My biggest concern, besides finding a foot in the pigpen, is what to do with the pigs when the authorities want to clear them out and look for any other remains that might be found in the mud." Her lips twisted. "I do have portable corral panels we used when we kept horses and cattle. We could set up a temporary structure to move them into."

"Are the panels sturdy enough to hold these guys?" Gerard's forehead puckered as his gaze swept over the pen full of pigs weighing over two hundred pounds.

Bernie nodded. "The panels are heavy-duty. They'll hold them long enough for the crime scene investigators to do their thing."

"What if they want to check the contents of their bellies for evidence?"

Bernie hadn't thought about that. "I'd planned on processing these hogs in a couple of weeks. It wouldn't hurt too much to send them to the slaughterhouse early."

"Do you name all your hogs?" Gerard asked.

Bernie shook her head. "Not the ones going to market." She tipped her head toward the pen. "Penelope is my breeding sow. The big guy in the corner is my breeding boar, Henry."

Gerard chuckled. "What famous Henry did you name him after?"

"It was a Hollywood toss-up between Henry

Winkler and Henry Cavill." She smiled. "But he proved early on that he's a king among swine."

"Henry the VIII," Gerard concluded.

Bernie nodded and looked back at the field of melons. "With the sheriff on his way, I'm sure they'll want me to hold off on harvesting my melons and produce. That concerns me more. I have to schedule my pickers well in advance. The crew that was supposed to come today will move on to their next job. I won't get them back until after everything has rotted in the fields."

"I might be able to help you with that. I know a handful of guys we could get out here as soon as the sheriff gives you the go-ahead."

"Good to know. Let's hope they don't take days for that to happen." She mounted the ATV, fired up the engine and gave Gerard a nod. Bernie goosed the throttle, sending the four-wheeler leaping forward. She turned around and headed for the house as sheriff's vehicles and an ambulance turned onto the road leading to her farm.

Deputy Shelby Taylor was the first to arrive. She waved at Bernie as she drove into the yard and pulled to a stop. When she got out of her service vehicle, she touched a hand to her flat belly. "Bernie, what's this I hear about you finding a body part in your pigpen?"

Bernie climbed off the four-wheeler, shaking her

head. "Just that. We found a foot in the pigpen a few minutes ago."

Shelby hugged Bernie. "It's been a while since I've been out to the farm. Seems the only time I see you is at the farmer's market. How've you been?"

Bernie shrugged. "Busy."

"I can only imagine." Shelby shook her head. "This place was a lot to manage when you and Ray were working it together."

"I'm doing okay as long as I don't get hit with major constraints like weather and, now...this." She stared at the deputy. "Speaking of busy, I was surprised to hear that you are—"

"Pregnant?" Shelby grinned, her hand resting on her still-flat belly. "No more surprised than we were. I'm only about a month along with eight more to go."

Bernie swallowed her envy, truly happy for her friend. When she'd married Ray, they'd talked of having four kids, starting their brood as soon as the farm started producing a steady income. The income came about the time Ray was diagnosed with ALS. Kids had ceased to be a part of their future. Hell, a future together stopped being a part of their young dreams. "Congratulations, Shelby."

"Thanks," the deputy said. "We're moving up our wedding date to accommodate our unexpected familial addition."

Sheriff Bergeron joined them while the ambulance crew dropped down from the cab and opened the rear of their truck.

"You won't need a gurney," Bernie said. "All we have is a foot."

The emergency medical technicians pulled on surgical gloves, grabbed a bag for the body part and joined the sheriff and deputy.

"I'd let you drive out to the pen, but it rained last night, and you might bog down in the mud," she said.

"Won't hurt us to walk," Sheriff Bergeron said. "Lead the way."

Bernie left the ATV in front of the house and led the entourage along the side of the field until they reached the pigpen on the far corner.

Gerard stood patiently guarding the foot. As they approached, he held out his hand. "Deputy Taylor, good to see you."

"Gerard…" She shook his hand. "Remy said he'd tagged you with this assignment. He thought it would be an easy one when all you had to do was find what or who killed Bernie's goose."

Gerard glanced down at the human foot. "I don't think it'll be as simple as he anticipated."

Bernie turned to the sheriff. "I don't know if you've had the chance to meet Sheriff Bergeron since you came to Bayou Mambaloa…?"

Gerard held out his hand to the sheriff. "I've seen

you in passing, but we haven't been formally introduced. Gerard Guidry."

The sheriff gripped his hand. "You're one of Remy Montagne's guys with the Bayou Brotherhood Protectors, right?"

Gerard nodded. "Yes, sir."

"Welcome to Bayou Mambaloa," the sheriff said and then squatted down to inspect the foot.

Deputy Taylor pulled a camera out of her pocket and started snapping photos of the foot and the pigpen.

"The state crime team is on its way," Sheriff Bergeron said. "They'll want to clear the pen of the livestock so they can look for the rest of the victim."

"In order to clear the pen, I'll need help moving corral panels into position," Bernie said.

"I gave my team a heads-up," Gerard said. "They're ready to help erect the temporary enclosure when we give them the word."

"Hopefully, the folks from the state crime lab will be here soon," the sheriff said. "They'll want to sweep the area around the pen before we trample any potential evidence." He glanced at the sky. "Won't be long before the sun sets. We'd like to get those pigs out of there before they trample any more body parts."

"I wouldn't be as concerned about them trampling parts as consuming them," Bernie said. "Pigs will eat any and everything—including human flesh and bones."

Deputy Taylor grimaced. "And to think, some people keep pigs as pets."

"While the sheriff and the crime scene investigators are working the area, could my guys help position the corral panels?" Gerard asked. "We can have them ready to move out here when they tell us it's okay."

Bernie nodded. "They don't need us here. Come on." She turned and started the long walk back across the field. "The panels are behind the barn. They'll need to be disassembled and loaded onto a trailer. I can hook the trailer up to the tractor to pull it out here."

Gerard kept pace with her. "I'll let the guys know to head this way." He pulled out his cell phone, keyed in a text and pressed SEND. A moment later, his phone pinged with a response. He glanced up. "They're on their way."

As they arrived at the barn, the Louisiana State crime scene team pulled into the yard at the same time as the truck loaded with her field workers.

Bernie pointed the crime scene team in the right direction and watched as they picked their way across the field. Then she turned to the man in charge of the workers and shook her head. "We won't be able to harvest today. I don't suppose you have room on your schedule to come back in two or three days?"

The weathered man shook his head and spoke with his heavy Hispanic accent, "I'm sorry, Ms. Bellamy. We were only scheduled to work this afternoon and tomorrow morning. We have to move on to the next job. It'll be a couple of weeks before we can get back here."

Bernie nodded. "I understand."

The men loaded into the truck and drove away.

Gerard stepped up beside her and touched her arm briefly. "It's okay. My team will see that your crop is harvested on time."

"Thanks," she said, at once grateful and frustrated that she had to rely on others to help her. She'd managed the last three years on her own and the two-and-a-half years before that when she'd taken care of Ray and the farm by herself. When she'd needed help, she'd contracted labor, refusing to be beholden to anyone. "I can only afford to pay them what I would've paid the crew that just left."

"They won't take your money. I think they'll actually look forward to working outside."

She pressed her lips together. "The melons are heavy, and the humidity makes it feel hotter than the air temperature."

"We've been working in the old boat factory, demolishing old, heavy equipment and then cleaning junk accumulated for decades. The place is big but not airconditioned." He glanced around. "It might be hot outside, but at least we have a chance at a breeze and sunshine on our faces."

Minutes later, a couple of trucks and an SUV pulled into the front yard and parked in a row. Several men dropped down from the vehicles and approached Bernie and Gerard. All were tall and muscular, but none quite as tall or broad-shouldered as Gerard.

A man with dark brown hair, reddish-brown eyes and a richly tanned complexion clapped a hand on Gerard's back. "First assignment, and you're already calling for reinforcements?"

Gerard glared at the man. "I just need you all for a few lousy minutes to help set up a temporary corral that'll hold some pigs."

"What do you need us to do?" A man with brown-black hair, smoky gray eyes and a sexy five-o'clock shadow turned on a smoldering hot smile and aimed it at Bernie.

That smile probably made other women weak at the knees. Bernie was startled at the faint flutter of awareness disturbing her gut.

She had to tell herself that the man had a great smile but was almost too handsome. And he probably knew it.

Bernie dragged her gaze away from the devastatingly handsome man and focused on Gerard.

Her assigned protector was a man whose face wore a scowl more often than a smile and who looked like he could rip a man's head off with his teeth. Well over six feet tall, his larger-than-life presence didn't intimidate her as she was sure he would other women. Instead, he was a calming influence that kept her grounded at the same time he kept her knotted inside.

When he'd touched her arm, she'd felt a shock of awareness. It had passed through her body like a lightning bolt, warming places that had been cold for too long, igniting a flame beneath her long-doused desire, making her want something more than the life she'd been living for the past three years.

As soon as the thought filled her brain, she realized how foolish it was to think a man like Gerard would be at all interested in a widow who spent ninety-nine percent of her time growing things and taking care of animals. She had little time for herself, much less anyone else. To pay her bills and keep food on the table, she had to work.

Besides, he'd only touched her arm out of a friendly concern. And surely it had been a fluke. A bodily reaction stemming from the stress of finding a foot on her property. What were the chances she'd have the same reaction if he touched her again?

Gerard leaned close and touched her arm again. "Bernie, are you all right?" His breath stirred the loose tendrils of hair around her ear, making her shiver with awareness.

When she didn't respond immediately, his hand found the small of her back.

Lightning ripped through her senses, blasting heat throughout her body, coiling tightly around her core. "I'm fine," she said, her voice breathy, not at all her usual firm, confident tone. "I'm just a little off balance by everything that's happened." She lifted her chin, squared her shoulders and shot a glance around at the men gathered around her in a semi-circle. "Follow me, and we can get started dismantling and loading the panels."

She led the men to the back side of the barn where the portable panels were standing where they'd been for the past four or five years. Weeds grew around them. What once had been a dirt lunging pen for horses was now filled with waist-high grass she hadn't bothered to mow because other chores took priority, like feeding animals, planting, tilling and harvesting crops.

Bernie waved a hand toward the panels. "There's a toolbox in the tack room. You'll need something to help you loosen the clamps holding the panels together. I'll bring the tractor and trailer around for you to stack the panels on." Bernie spun on her heels and headed into the barn.

Gerard followed, his mere presence keeping her pulse racing erratically. She couldn't function this way. She needed distance between herself and Gerard.

Bernie stopped. "You don't have to help me. I can do this myself. I've hooked up utility trailers to the tractor and my trucks for years. I can almost do it with my eyes closed." Okay, that was stretching the truth a bit. She just didn't want him to dog her every footstep or touch her again.

He was little more than a stranger, and she shouldn't be feeling anything but gratitude for his kindness.

They had bigger problems than her non-existent sex life. She had a crop to harvest and a mystery to solve.

She didn't have time to moon over a giant of a man who made her feel again.

He needed to go away and let her get her head on straight. She didn't need a protector. The sheriff's department and state crime lab would be enough to solve this case.

She wasn't even sure who or what she was supposed to be kept safe from.

So, they'd found a foot in the pigpen. That didn't automatically equate to danger to herself or her animals. She had a rifle, a shotgun and a handgun, and she wasn't afraid to use them.

As soon as the state crime lab team left, she'd send Gerard on his way and get her life back on its normal track.

Usually an optimist, the series of events Bernie had endured over the past five or six years had left her cautious and determined to be independent. She never wanted to depend on a man for physical contact or emotional support. It had hurt too much when she'd lost Ray. Bernie wasn't sure she would survive another such loss.

In her mind, it was settled. Once they had the pigs moved into the temporary corral, Gerard could leave. Then Bernie could get back to her life and quit having those flashes of heat stealing through her every time he touched her. In time, she might stop craving those touches.

CHAPTER 3

GERARD RETRIEVED the tools from the barn and went to work with his team dismantling the corral panels.

Bernie disappeared for a few minutes. The rumbling sound of an engine starting made Gerard abandon the team and go in search of her.

Though she'd insisted she could hitch the trailer to the tractor by herself, Gerard knew from experience it was easier to hook up a trailer with two people—one driving, the other directing from the ground.

He found Bernie perched on an ancient red tractor, making a circle in the barnyard. She slowed to a stop, shifted gears into reverse and backed toward a long flatbed trailer parked in the middle of a row of various tractor implements.

Gerard hurried forward and stopped beside the trailer hitch. "A little more to your left," he called out.

She adjusted her direction accordingly, backing slowly toward him until she was as close as he needed to match the trailer hitch to the ball on the back of the tractor.

Gerard pulled the hitch, trailer and all, until it was directly over the ball and cranked the handle, lowering the trailer hitch until it covered the ball. He continued cranking until the jack beneath the hitch was up as high as it would go. Then he locked the hitch in place, stepped back and gave Bernie a thumbs-up.

While she drove the tractor and trailer around to the back of the barn, he kept pace on foot, arriving at the same time.

Gerard and his team stacked the heavy metal panels onto the trailer one by one. When they were done, they followed the tractor and trailer to the front of the barn.

Lucas brushed dust from his shirt and jeans. "I'm glad we didn't change clothes after finishing up at the boat factory."

"Same," Beau said.

Gerard stood beside his new boss, Remy Montagne. "Did Shelby give you an idea of who the foot might belong to?"

Remy shook his head. "Haven't heard a thing. I'm

not sure she knows I'm here. I just walked into the Crawdad Hole when you called to say you needed our help." His lips twisted. "Who knew a dead goose would lead to a foot in a pigpen." Remy frowned. "Speak of the devil."

A lone figure dressed in a uniform tromped across the field toward them.

Gerard recognized Deputy Shelby Taylor, making her way around the watermelon patch.

Remy hurried forward to greet his fiancée with a kiss. "Hey, babe, how are you holding up?"

She leaned into him for a moment. "I'll be glad when I get past the first trimester. I'm always so tired."

"The doctor said your body is adjusting to your pregnancy." Remy tucked a stray strand of hair behind her ear.

"I know," she sighed. "But the nausea...and the smell from the pigpen." She covered her mouth with her hand. "It was all I could do not to lose my lunch."

"You're due to get off in…" Remy glanced down at his watch, "thirty-five minutes."

She nodded. "I can last that long."

Bernie climbed down from the tractor and joined Remy, Shelby and Gerard. "Did they find anything else near the pigpen?"

Shelby shook her head. "No, but Sheriff Bergeron said last night's shift on the bayou was looking for illegal fishing and 'gator hunters and ran across a couple of guys carrying guns near the shore not far from here. When the deputy called out for them to raise their hands, they shot at the deputy."

"Did the deputy get hurt?" Bernie asked.

Shelby frowned. "No. He landed his boat and chased after the men on foot."

"Did he catch them?" Remy asked.

"No." Shelby sighed. "They got away in a vehicle. The deputy didn't get close enough to get the plate number. On his way back to his boat, he found another car half-sunk in the bayou. He ran the plates and discovered they had been stolen in New Orleans earlier that evening. They've dusted the car for prints. We're still waiting to hear if they found a match."

"Might be the foot's owner," Gerard said. "The guys who got away could've put him in the pigpen."

"That's what we're thinking," Deputy Taylor said. "We'll know more if we get a hit on the prints. The crime team said you can set up the temporary pen now. They need to get into the pen to continue their search."

Bernie's gaze met Gerard's.

His pulse quickened, and heat flooded his groin. Not good. He couldn't get hot and bothered by this woman. She was his client.

"Ready?" Bernie asked.

Boy, was he. Gerard tamped down his reaction to her and nodded. "We'll follow you out there."

She turned and hurried to the tractor, climbed into the seat and shifted into gear. The tractor lurched forward, jerking the trailer along with it.

Remy frowned down at his fiancée. "Are you coming?"

She covered her nose and mouth, shaking her head. "No way. I barely kept my stomach down the first time. I'm heading back to the station to work on my report and see if they've come up with a match on the fingerprints." She leaned up on her toes and brushed her lips across his. "I'll see you later."

"You call that a kiss?" Remy caught her around her waist and captured her mouth in a crushing kiss before turning her loose. "Better?"

Shelby swayed. "Much. As long as Sheriff Bergeron didn't witness that. He read me the riot act about public displays of affection in uniform." Shelby looked past Remy. "Good thing he's otherwise occupied with the crime scene investigators." She shot Remy a stern glance. "Don't do that again unless you want to get me fired."

Remy held up both hands. "I definitely don't want to get you fired. You know how I love a woman in uniform." He growled low in his chest. "Especially when I get to help her out of that uniform."

Gerard coughed. "Seriously? You two need to get a room."

"We have one," Remy and Shelby answered simultaneously and laughed.

"Later," Deputy Taylor said.

Gerard followed the trailer. His team fell in step with him, Remy on one side, Lucas on the opposite. The others trailed behind.

"Your mission has gone from the murder of a goose to the mystery of a human foot missing its body." Lucas walked beside Gerard. "Makes your assignment more interesting."

Gerard shrugged. "What gets me is that the goose had a broken neck, yet it ended up on Bernie's front porch."

"How did a goose with a broken neck get onto her front porch?" Beau asked.

Gerard snorted. "Good question. If someone murdered the man who's missing his foot, why risk being caught putting a dead goose on her front porch?"

"Could it be that the goose and the foot are unrelated?" Valentin asked.

"Maybe," Gerard said.

"She's not an heiress or a princess in hiding, but she's not bad-looking," Romeo commented from behind Gerard. "Is your client married?"

Gerard shot a frown at his teammate. "Widowed."

"Ah, a widow." Romeo's eyebrows rose. "Recent?"

"Leave her alone." Gerard glared at his friend. "She's got enough on her plate. She doesn't need you stalking her. Not only does she have to deal with a potential murder on her property..." Gerard waved at the field of watermelons, "these watermelons have to be harvested in the next day or two, or they'll rot on the vines. Her pickers were supposed to pick today but couldn't do the work with the place being turned into a crime scene."

"Are they coming tomorrow?" Remy asked.

Gerard shook his head. "They can't get back to her farm for three weeks."

"Which means her crop will rot in the field," Lucas concluded.

Gerard hadn't yet brought up his offer to have his team harvest the melons. Now was the perfect segue into that topic. "Not if she finds another crew of pickers to bring them in."

Romeo's eyes narrowed. "Where are you going with this, man?"

Gerard shrugged. "I have an assignment. What do you have?" He turned to the others. "What do any of you have to occupy your time now?"

Remy grinned. "Nothing, yet. We aren't needed at the boat factory. The contractor will begin work on Monday, and we'll just be in the way. We can harvest those melons for Ms. Bellamy."

A collective groan sounded from the rest of the men.

Gerard's lips twitched but managed to keep from grinning. He'd hoped Remy would make it sound like his idea. Gerard would help harvest whether or not the others decided to help.

"I'll get more information from Bernie—Ms. Bellamy—about how we should go about picking watermelons," Gerard offered.

"After we erect a pigpen," Romeo grumbled.

"Join Brotherhood Protectors..." Beau said.

"Save the world..." Valentin added, "one pig at a time."

The men were still chuckling when Bernie brought the tractor to a stop near the pigpen.

"Wow." Lucas covered his mouth and nose. "I say we get this pen up as quickly as we can."

Beau dragged the collar of his T-shirt up over his nose. "I second that motion."

Bernie shut off the engine and climbed down from the tractor. "Sorry, guys. I'm past due for cleaning out the pen, and it rained recently. Of course, the pigs love the mud, but it compounds the odor." She gave them instructions on how and where to construct the panels to form an enclosure for the herd of swine.

With the help of his team, Gerard was pleased

with how quickly they got the pen up and the animals moved into it.

Once the job was done, Bernie double-checked the enclosure, tugging on the panels to make sure they wouldn't give way if bumped by a four-hundred-pound hog. Her smooth brow dented. "It will have to do. And I'll have time to clean their pen after the crime scene team finishes their investigation."

"Clean their pen?" Gerard asked.

"I go in with the tractor and front-end loader and scoop out all the yuckiness, deposit it in the compost pile at the opposite end of the pen and use the natural fertilizer on my field." She clapped her hands together. "That will have to wait until after I harvest the melons."

"Looks like you'll have a little help," Gerard said.

Her brow wrinkled. "Oh yeah? Who?"

Remy stepped forward. "My team of Brotherhood Protectors would like to assist you in bringing in your crop of watermelons, Ms. Bellamy."

She shook her head. "It's back-breaking work," she warned.

"We're all strong and ready to help," their leader said. "All you have to do is let us know how you want it done and where to load all the watermelons."

"Are you sure?" she asked, a frown pinching the skin over the bridge of her nose.

"If you'd rather we didn't—" Romeo started.

Gerard elbowed the man in the gut. "What my friend here meant is we'd be glad to help. Right, Romeo?"

Romeo pressed a hand to his belly. "Yes, ma'am," he said through gritted teeth as he doubled over. "Looking forward to helping out."

A smile spread slowly across Bernie's face, changing her from plain to beautiful. The late afternoon sunshine added to her glow. "Thank you." She turned to Gerard and kissed his cheek. "Thank you."

His breath caught as her lips brushed across his skin. Heat rose up his neck and sank down into his groin. For a moment, he couldn't put two words together to form anything that would make sense.

"Hey, we're all going to help, not just Gerard," Romeo said and turned his face to the side, presenting his cheek.

Gerard glared at his friend.

Before he could say anything, Remy clapped his hands together. "When do you want to start?"

Bernie stared out at the field of melons. "If we start now, we can get through half the field tonight and finish the other half tomorrow after the morning dew has burned off. That will give me time to deliver the first load to my distributor in New Orleans and get back. Then we can finish loading the rest tomorrow afternoon. We should be finished well before dark, in time for me to take the second load to New Orleans."

Beau raised a hand to shade his eyes. "How many melons do you think you have here?"

"I planted one acre at a projected yield of about fifteen tons per acre. I'm not sure how much damage Penelope did."

"Penelope?" Lucas asked.

"One of her pigs," Gerard said.

"My breeder sow," Bernie added. "As for how many melons are out there..." She tipped her head to one side and narrowed her eyes. "At maybe 50-100 melons per ton, there should be around a thousand melons or more, minus the ones Penelope destroyed on her midnight binge."

Gerard blinked. "A thousand?"

She nodded. "My pickers would've harvested them all today had they been allowed to start when they arrived earlier. I had the boxes ready and waiting. All we have to do is load the boxes onto this trailer, and we can start—if your guys are serious."

"Oh, we're serious," Remy said. "Aren't we, team?"

"Sure," Jacques said.

Romeo grumbled under his breath before saying, "Right. Who doesn't love watermelon?"

Sin planted his hands on his hips. "Where do we start?"

"A couple of you can help me load the cardboard

boxes onto the trailer. The rest can begin picking and lining the melons up, ready to put them in the boxes when we get back with the trailer."

"How do we know which melons to pick?" Sin asked.

"Follow me." Bernie walked out among the watermelon vines.

Gerard admired the woman's no-nonsense approach to farming and the way she patiently showed the men how to determine if a melon was ripe enough to pick. She pulled a pocketknife out of her jeans pocket and sliced through a stem. She held up her pocketknife. "Who needs a knife?"

Each man pulled a knife from a scabbard on his belt and flipped it open.

Bernie chuckled. "Always prepared, huh? You all must have been good Boy Scouts."

"No, ma'am," Remy said. "Navy SEAL, here."

She grinned.

The way her face lit up made Gerard's blood run hot through his veins.

"All right," Bernie crossed her arms over her chest. "Remy, show me a ripe melon."

One by one, she had each guy identify a ripe melon before she turned them loose to start picking.

When she was satisfied they knew a ripe melon from a green one, Bernie climbed onto the tractor, turned it around and headed for the barn.

Gerard, Remy and Landry followed. At the barn, they loaded large, sturdy cardboard boxes onto the flatbed trailer and rode with them back out to the field.

Valentin, Romeo and Beau turned out to be the best at picking the ripe melons. They passed the melons in bucket-brigade style from one man to the next, handing the heavy fruit up to Gerard and Bernie, who then set them gently into the cardboard boxes until each box was full.

The work was strenuous, the heat and humidity making them sweat. By the time the trailer was full, Gerard was tired, his muscles sore, and he was ready for a shower, a beer and food, but not necessarily in that order. He jumped down from his position on the trailer and stretched his arms above his head, working the kinks out of his back.

Bernie drove the tractor back to the barn, pulling the heavily loaded trailer along behind her. She'd worked as hard as the rest of them without once grumbling about the heat, the backbreaking task or the fact that they had to do it all again the next day.

Gerard suspected his teammates had stopped grumbling when they'd realized Bernie was keeping up with them without complaint.

And to think, she'd been running the farm single-handed. Gerard's respect for the woman ratcheted up significantly. He walked with his team back to the barn behind the tractor and helped Bernie unhitch the trailer from the tractor and hitch it to her truck for the drive into New Orleans the following morning.

Bernie nodded toward the house. "There's beer in the refrigerator in the kitchen. Help yourself. I have a huge pot of gumbo already cooked. All I have to do is warm it up if you'd like to stay for dinner."

"You don't have to go to the trouble," Remy said. "We can get something to eat in town."

"And leave me with all that gumbo?" Bernie shook her head. "I made it for the pickers. I always provide a meal for them when they come. I make a pretty decent gumbo if I say so myself."

"Count me in." Romeo rubbed his belly. "I could eat a whole pig after that workout."

"Shh." Lucas grinned. "Don't let Penelope hear you say that. She might take offense."

"It shouldn't take me fifteen minutes to warm it up," Bernie said. "I have plenty of beer in the refrigerator for those interested and bottled water for everyone else."

Gerard followed her into the kitchen, grabbed the case of beer she had chilling in the fridge and carried it out to the team.

The men took turns rinsing their hands and faces under the spigot at the side of the house. Once they'd dripped dry, they each grabbed a beer from the case and settled on the porch steps, the swing or leaned against the railing, sipping beer and poking fun at each other.

"I think Delta Force training was easier than harvesting a field of watermelons," Lucas said, rolling his shoulders.

Sin shook his head. "I don't know what Delta Force training you went through, man, but it couldn't have been the same as mine."

"I don't know," Beau said. "We'd only loaded one box with melons when I started looking for a bell to ring."

Gerard laughed with the rest of the men, remembering how many of his fellow trainees had rung the bell, signaling the end of their training, having given up. Even at his worst, he'd never considered quitting. He'd suffered worse at the hands of his father. Delta Force training had been a walk in the park.

Dusk was settling on the farm when the crime scene investigators wrapped up their work in the pig enclosure and made their way back to their vehicles parked in the barnyard.

While the investigators loaded into their cars and drove away, Sheriff Bergeron stepped onto the porch.

Bernie came out of the kitchen, wiping her hands on the sides of her jeans. "Well? Did they find anything else?"

The sheriff sighed. "Not much. Definitely no

more body parts." He pulled out his cell phone and brought up a photo. "They used a metal detector and found a men's silver ring in the muck." He passed his cell phone to Bernie. "Do you recognize this ring?"

Bernie studied the image, her brow furrowing. "It's not mine. I doubt it was my husband's. He never wore any kind of jewelry. He refused to wear a wedding band because he worked around so much farm machinery, and he didn't want to get one caught in anything and lose a finger." She tipped her head, her frown deepening. "The symbol is a fleur-de-lis."

"It was inscribed on the inside." The sheriff scrolled to another photo.

"I can barely make out the letters," Bernie said.

Gerard leaned over Bernie's shoulder. After a second or two, he read it out loud. *"Je t'aime.* It's French for I love you." As he realized just how close he was to Bernie, Gerard's pulse beat faster. Heat burned through his body that had nothing to do with the oppressive humidity and air temperature.

Bernie turned her head, her face mere inches from his. Her eyes flared, and her cheeks pinkened,

Gerard's breath lodged in his chest. He took a quick step backward, putting a safe distance between himself and his client.

"I've seen those words before..." Bernie whispered. "And that symbol." She covered her mouth with her hand and closed her eyes. "But where?" A moment later, her eyes popped open, and she dove for the door, disappearing into the farmhouse.

Gerard assumed she'd just remembered that she had food on the stove and had gone inside to check on it.

"How was the watermelon picking?" the sheriff asked.

A collective groan rose from the men on the porch.

Sheriff Bergeron chuckled. "You made good progress, considering you got a late start this afternoon. I remember working one summer for a farmer who grew watermelons and cantaloupes. That's why I chose to go into law enforcement."

"I have a whole new respect for the men and women who do this for a living," Remy said.

The sheriff grinned. "I'll bet you do."

Bernie stepped out onto the porch. "I thought I'd seen that symbol and inscription before. It finally dawned on me where." She held out her hand and dropped a necklace into the sheriff's palm. "This was my mother's necklace. She wore it all the time. She gave it to me before she died."

The necklace was a simple silver chain with a pendant bearing the fleur-de-lis symbol on one side.

When the sheriff turned it over, Gerard could see the same inscription on the back of the pendant as was on the inside of the ring.

The sheriff held the necklace next to the image on his phone. "Was your mother ever near the pigpen?"

Bernie shook her head. "I didn't marry Ray until after my mother passed. As far as I know, she never visited Bellamy Farm."

"Hmm." Sheriff Bergeron's lips pressed together. "Do you mind if I take this into evidence? I promise you'll get it back. This is too much of a coincidence."

"Of course," Bernie said. "And yes, it's too much of a coincidence. Why would a ring matching the necklace my mother wore end up in a pigpen she'd never come near?"

"Good question." The sheriff pulled an evidence bag out of his pocket, deposited the necklace inside and nodded at Bernie. "I'm sorry this is all coming at a bad time, with harvest and all."

Bernie's lips twisted. "Is there ever a good time to find a foot in your pigpen?"

"No," the sheriff said. "If I hear anything useful, I'll let you know. In the meantime, lock your doors and carry a gun."

"Yes, sir," Bernie said.

"I can have a unit check on your place periodically," he pushed a hand through his hair. "Sorry, but I don't have the staff to post someone here twenty-four-seven."

"Sir," Gerard stepped forward. "We've got Ms. Bellamy covered."

The sheriff frowned. "We?" He turned toward Remy. "As in your team? The Brotherhood Protectors?"

Remy nodded. "Gerard will be with her twenty-four-seven until this situation is resolved."

"Excellent." Sheriff Bergeron smiled at Bernie. "Remy and Gerard proved themselves keeping Deputy Taylor and her family safe when a drug cartel tried to set up shop in our neighborhood. You're in good hands."

Bernie shot a quick glance in Gerard's direction, her cheeks turning a pretty shade of pink. "Mr. Guidry has already been a big help on the farm. I'm afraid I'm taking advantage of him."

Gerard shook his head. "Not at all. Anything I can do to help."

She grinned. "You might regret those words when you get up tomorrow morning, sore as hell from lifting hundreds of watermelons."

He suspected he'd hurt, but he had no regrets. This woman needed help on the farm and keeping her safe from whoever had disposed of a body in a pigpen. Well, at least a foot.

"I hope your evening improves," the sheriff said.

"It already has," Bernie responded with a smile. "Half of my crop is ready to market despite losing my pickers today."

Her happiness made Gerard's aching back worth

the pain. He liked the way her face glowed when she was happy and wanted to be the one who brought out that glow.

"I'm glad to hear it," Sheriff Bergeron said. "Let us know if you find anything interesting while harvesting the remainder of your field."

Bernie nodded. "Will do."

After the sheriff drove off, Bernie dashed into the house to rescue the warming gumbo.

Seconds later, she came back through the door, her face white.

Gerard hurried forward and gripped her arm. "What's wrong?"

She raised her hand and stared down at the cell phone in her palm. "I got a text message from an unknown caller."

He took the cell phone from her.

Remy and the other men on the porch gathered around as he read the message aloud.

WE WANT WHAT YOU HAVE

GIVE IT UP OR DIE

CHAPTER 4

BERNIE SHIVERED. Hearing the words aloud had an even more frightening effect than reading them on her cell phone.

"Phone number?" Remy asked.

Gerard shook his head in unison with Bernie. "Unknown caller."

Remy pulled his own cell phone from his pocket and punched in a number. "Swede," he said. "Our client just received a death threat via text. Can you hack into an unknown caller?" Remy nodded. "I understand, but if it leads to something other than a burner phone..." His gaze met Bernie's. "I'll shoot you her phone number in a text. Anything you can do could help. Thanks." He ended the call.

"Who's Swede?" Bernie asked.

"Axel Svenson," Remy said, "aka Swede, is the Brotherhood Protectors' technical expert at our home office in Montana. Do you mind if I share your phone number with him? He might have some connections to access your phone records and maybe trace the text back to its source."

"Share it. Anything you need. I use the same phone number for personal and business use. It's not a secret." Bernie frowned. "You said something about a burner phone. Can he trace one of those?"

"Probably not," Remy said as he scrolled through his contacts list and shared Bernie's phone number with the technical expert. "But if it isn't a burner phone, we might have a chance of identifying the sender. In the meantime, you need twenty-four-seven protection."

"You think this guy is serious?" Bernie wrapped her arms around her middle, suddenly cold in the heat of southern Louisiana.

Gerard handed her cell phone back to her. "Do you want to take a chance that he's not?"

Bernie shook her head. "I just hate to be a bother. And I'm pretty sure I can't afford to pay Brotherhood Protectors for twenty-four-seven security."

"Don't worry about payment," Remy said. "Hank Patterson, our founder, doesn't take on clients based on their ability to pay. He and his wife, Sadie

McClain, set up the funding to offer services to anyone who needs it, regardless of their ability to pay."

Bernie frowned. "Sadie McClain. That name sounds familiar."

Gerard grinned. "It should. She's one of Hollywood's biggest movie stars."

Bernie's eyes rounded. "Sadie McClain, the movie star? Wow. That's very generous of her and her husband."

Remy turned to Gerard. "Since Gerard had initially been sent on this particular assignment, it only makes sense that he be the one to stay."

Bernie met Gerard's gaze.

He gave a subtle nod.

Remy continued. "The other alternative is to stay with Shelby and me. Or at the Bayou Brotherhood Boarding House."

Before Remy finished talking, Bernie was already shaking her head. "I can't leave the animals. I've already lost my beloved Gertrude and could've lost Penelope. I can't leave the animals to fend for themselves."

"Then, it's settled," Gerard said. "I'm staying."

"Any idea what the text message sender was referring to when he said you have what he wants?" Gerard asked.

Bernie raised her hands, palms turned upward, looking around at her home, the house, the barn, and the animals in the pasture. "No. The only thing new around here was the foot we found. I can't imagine that's what he wanted." She drew a deep breath and let it out slowly, her gaze returning to Gerard. "All I know is I'm going to burn the gumbo if I don't turn off the burner on the stove. Death threat aside, dinner's ready."

Gerard looked down at his dirty shirt and jeans. "Though we washed what we could, we're still too dirty to sit at the table."

Bernie waved her hand. "So am I. The farmhouse kitchen was designed to seat a dozen workers. The table is huge, and you can't hurt the chairs. The bottom line is, we can all eat in the kitchen."

The men followed her into the kitchen.

"Sit," she ordered.

Romeo popped to attention and saluted. "Yes, ma'am." Then he winked and dropped into one of the wooden chairs. The others followed suit.

It was nice to have company in the big kitchen. When she ate alone, the table stretched out so long and empty that she took her food into the living room and turned on the television, more for the noise than because she wanted to watch anything.

Bernie scooped heaping ladles full of the chicken

and shrimp gumbo into bowls. Her hands still shook after reading the death threat on her cell phone.

Gerard appeared at her side. "Are you all right?"

No. She wasn't. Why was this happening to her?

She gave him a watery smile. "I'm fine."

He leaned close, touching a hand to the small of her back, and whispered. "I'll keep you safe."

Warmth spread throughout her along with the sudden urge to cry. The lump in her throat wouldn't let air past her vocal cords. All she could do was nod and hand him two bowls of gumbo.

He carried bowls to the table as fast as she could fill them.

When everyone had a bowl in front of them, Bernie poured the rest of the gumbo into a tureen. Gerard carried it to the table and set it in the center.

Once everyone had gumbo, Bernie joined the men, carrying a basket of cornbread muffins. As she approached the table, Gerard pulled out her chair and held it as she took the seat.

With all eyes on her, she forced herself to take up her spoon, even though eating was the last thing on her mind. With Gerard on one side and Remy on the other, she felt safe. For the moment.

The meal began with the men handing around the basket of muffins and the bottle of Tabasco sauce. Soon, the Brotherhood Protectors team, who'd spent the afternoon loading heavy watermelons onto the trailer, talked, joked, laughed and compared aches and pains.

Bernie relaxed and even ate a few bits of gumbo and half a muffin.

"Compliments to the chef," Romeo said after eating half his bowl of the steamy stew. "Best gumbo I've ever had. Even better than my grandmother's." He frowned. "Don't tell her. I might lose my status as the favorite grandson."

Bernie stared across the table at Romeo, her expression serious. "Thank you. Your secret is safe with me. I would never break an old woman's heart."

Romeo grinned. "Ms. Bellamy, you might just be the woman of my dreams."

She shook her head. "How can that be? You've only just met me."

"You've got a helluva a green thumb, you can drive a tractor and make gumbo that belongs in one of those fancy Cajun restaurants in New Orleans. Best of all, you're kindhearted." Romeo tipped his chin toward Gerard. "Don't go fallin' in love with ol' Grouchy Gerard before you give me a chance."

Bernie forced a laugh, her cheeks burning.

"You can't have all the pretty girls, Romeo," Beau said. "Besides, I thought you were into the pretty shopkeeper?"

"What shopkeeper?" Bernie asked.

"The one with the gift shop," Beau offered. "What's her name? Elizabeth?"

Romeo frowned. "Her name is Giselle." He gave Bernie a crooked smile. "Can I help it I love women?"

Bernie shook her head. "I'm flattered but not interested. No offense," she assured him. "I just don't have time for a relationship. I have a farm to run."

"It's a lot of work for—" Gerard started and stopped.

"A woman?" Bernie finished, her lips twisting.

He shook his head. "I was going to say *for one person*. You worked every bit as hard, if not harder, than any one of us. It's just a lot to handle by yourself."

She sighed. "It's my livelihood. If I don't do it, I can't afford to keep the lights on, the animals in feed and taxes paid on the land. Or I'd have to find a job." Bernie laughed. "This is a small town. There aren't that many jobs available. That's why so many young people leave after high school. I'd have to go to New Orleans or Baton Rouge to find work that would pay enough to support me and my menagerie. And who—"

"—would take care of the animals while you worked in the city?" Gerard nodded. "I get it."

"Have you thought about selling the place and using the money to start over somewhere else?" Landry asked.

Gerard's lips twitched. "She has."

Bernie frowned. "Brokers representing the Grand Bijou Golf Resort Corporation would love nothing better than for me to sell this property to them. And they'd pay enough I wouldn't have to find a job for a long time, if at all." She tipped her head toward Gerard. "You know how I feel."

Gerard turned to his team. "She's not selling."

Remy's eyes narrowed. "You have something they want."

Bernie's eyes widened. "Do you think they'd go to the extreme of threatening me to get me to sell?"

Remy shrugged. "It's worth checking into. What did you say was the name of the corporation?"

"Grand Bijou Golf Resort," Bernie repeated.

Remy keyed the name into his cell phone. "Did you get the name of the Brokerage firm?"

"Worthington Brokerage out of Miami." Bernie pushed back from the table and stood.

The men came to their feet at the same time.

"You don't have to get up," Bernie said. "Finish your meal."

Gerard glanced around at the others. "I think we're done."

Bernie shrugged and crossed to the counter, where she dropped mail and documents that needed to be sorted and filed. She sifted through the stack that had gotten ridiculously deep until she found the business card and handed it to Remy.

"They sent a couple of their brokers out. I had a hard time getting rid of them. They didn't want to take no for an answer. They need to close a deal on Bellamy Acres before they can begin construction. I think they assumed it would be an easy deal. Offer me enough money, and me being a widow, I'd be glad to sell."

"I'll have Swede check into the resort and the brokerage firm," Remy said.

The guys gathered their dishes and carried them to the sink.

"Don't worry about the dishes. I'll take care of them," Bernie said.

"No, ma'am," Gerard said. "You cooked. We can clean." He washed bowls and stacked them neatly into the dish drainer while his teammates cleared the table and helped put away the leftovers.

Unused to having others do the work for her, Bernie grabbed a towel and dried the dishes Gerard washed. Occasionally, Gerard's arm brushed against hers, sending a burst of electricity through her system.

In no time at all, the bowls were stacked in the cabinet, utensils were in the drawer and the table was cleared and clean.

Bernie followed the men as they headed out the door and down the porch steps. All of them but one.

While most of the men piled into the vehicles parked between the house and barn, Remy paused at the bottom of the stairs. "When will you be back from the city?"

"No later than noon," Bernie said. "If your men show up at twelve-thirty, I'll have the trailer positioned in the field, ready to go."

Remy nodded. "We'll be there." He turned to Gerard. "You need anything from the boarding house?"

Gerard shook his head. "I keep some basics in the storage compartment on my motorcycle."

"And I'm sure I can find anything else you might need here to tide you over until we're on our way back through town tomorrow," Bernie said. "We can stop by the boarding house to gather anything else then."

Gerard nodded.

"Then we're out of here," Remy said. "Call if you need anything or run into any trouble."

"Will do," Gerard said.

Moments later, the vehicles departed, taillights disappearing into the darkness, leaving Bernie alone with Gerard.

"I'll be right back," Gerard descended the stairs

and crossed to where he'd parked his motorcycle beneath a tree.

Bernie shivered in the balmy night air, her thoughts pouring over the day's events, starting with finding Gertrude dead on her front porch and ending with a man staying the night with her. The stuff in between was what nightmares were made of. Finding a human foot and receiving a death threat didn't happen every day.

As Gerard turned around and strode across the yard in her direction, another shiver rippled through Bernie's body. This time, it was not from the startling and frightening events of the day but the sudden quickening of her pulse at the sight of the Marine's broad shoulders and confident stride, eating the distance between them.

The closer he came, the more ragged her breathing became until she found herself holding her breath.

Gerard climbed the steps, his large frame towering over her, a small backpack in his hands.

Bernie didn't consider herself a small woman. At five-foot-ten, she could look most men straight in the eye.

Not Gerard.

With him standing so close, she had to tilt her head back to meet his gaze.

He frowned down at her. "Are you okay?"

She let go of the breath she'd been holding. "Yes, of course," she said, cursing inwardly at how breathy she sounded. "Why do you ask?"

"As I walked up to you, you looked...scared." His frown deepened. "I hope you're not scared of me. I promise I would never hurt you."

She pressed a hand to her throat, afraid he could see how swiftly her pulse was beating and that he would guess that his nearness was the cause.

"I'm not afraid of you," she said, avoiding the truth. She was afraid of her body's reaction to him. The man awakened something deep inside her that she thought had died with her husband.

Raw, searing, hot desire.

Like a heater turned up full blast, her body burned from the inside out, radiating heat from every pore, an inferno blazing at her core.

"Are you sure you're all right?" Gerard asked. "You look..."

Hot? Sex-starved? Desperate?

Sweet Jesus, she had to get a grip. "I look like I need a shower?" She forced a laugh. "Yes. I do. I think I'll get that shower. Now." She spun on her heels and marched her horny ass into the house, down the hall-way, through the master bedroom and into the bath-room. After she closed the door, she turned and locked it. Not to keep him out but to keep her from begging him to join her.

She pressed her palms to her burning cheeks. "What is wrong with me?"

She was tired. That was it.

And stressed.

Who wouldn't be after finding body parts and death threats? Her lust could be a way for her body to distract her from the real issues.

She reached into the shower and turned on the water, leaving it all the way in the cold position, determined to douse the errant flame before it burned out of control. Then she shed her clothes, dropping them on the floor around her feet.

For a moment, she stood naked, letting herself imagine what out-of-control might manifest into.

Like marching naked out of the bathroom and throwing herself at the man whose job was to protect her.

Or calling out to him for help and then trapping him in the bathroom, where she would strip his clothes off and run her hands all over his body.

Bernie moaned. "Enough."

She stepped beneath the shower's spray and gasped. Cold water pelted her skin. For several long minutes, she fought to catch her breath, gooseflesh pebbling her skin.

Slowly, the heat abated, leaving her shivering in the cold spray.

Relieved that the cool water had done the trick,

she turned the handle, adding warm water to the shower head. Then she worked shampoo into her hair and soaped her body, washing away the dirt and grime normal for a day's hard work on the farm. She ran her hands over her neck and arms, across her breasts and downward to the juncture of her thighs.

And just like that, she was on fire all over again.

Twisting the handle back to cold, she stood under the punishingly cold spray until all the suds disappeared down the drain, along with her desire, and she was clean.

Bernie shut off the water, grabbed a towel and attacked her skin, rubbing harder than necessary to dry herself.

She wrapped the towel around her and pushed the door open just enough so she could see through to the living room.

Damn. She'd left the bedroom door open.

She hadn't brought a change of clothes into the bathroom with her. Which meant she had to pass in front of the bedroom door to reach her dresser with her clothes inside.

If Gerard happened to see her in her bedroom, wrapped only in a towel, so what? All the important parts were covered. She had nothing to be afraid of.

Unless her fingers slipped and the towel fell to the bedroom floor, exposing her naked body to the Marine.

Bernie tiptoed across the floor, holding the towel in one hand as she reached for the door to close it.

As her hand connected with the doorknob, Gerard appeared in front of her. "Oh," he said. "Sorry. I was just going to check to see if you were okay." His gaze swept over her in a brief sweep from head to toe. "You look...okay." He swallowed, the muscles in his neck contracting. "I'll just leave you to finish." Gerard grabbed the doorknob and pulled the door closed between them.

For a long moment, Bernie stared at the door, willing it to open again so that she could drop the towel and throw herself at the man.

The door didn't open.

She dropped the towel anyway and debated whether to wear a bra or not. Usually, she didn't wear one at night. She opted for the bra, not wanting Gerard to think she was coming on to him. Then she grabbed a T-shirt from one of her drawers and a pair of stretchy shorts. Once dressed, she stared at the door again.

If she were smart, she'd leave the door closed and go to bed, avoiding temptation.

Yeah. Well, she wasn't smart, and it wasn't very late. If she went to bed now, she'd lay awake staring at the ceiling. She might as well watch TV in the living room and quit fanaticizing about sex with her bodyguard.

After dragging a brush through her hair, smoothing out all the tangles, she sucked in a breath and marched for the door.

Her hand on the knob, she breathed in, held it...

A knock sounded on the door, startling Bernie.

She let go of the breath she'd just sucked in, yanked open the door and faced the man who'd been on her mind for half the day.

He grinned and held up a bowl of popcorn. "Care to watch a movie with me?"

She frowned. "Depends on the movie." That was a lie. He was asking if she wanted to watch a movie with him. Her answer was yes. The movie didn't matter in the least. Unless it was a horror movie with things that jumped out at them and made her have nightmares. In that case, she would have to sit quietly with her eyes closed throughout.

"It's a romantic comedy," he offered with a smile.

"Couldn't you find an action-adventure movie?" Bernie asked.

"I thought you'd like to watch something light and funny to take your mind off some of the day's events."

"Light and funny wouldn't keep my mind engaged. I need action, fight scenes, dodging in and out of trouble, being surprised at every corner." She grinned. "That will keep my mind off today's revelations."

Gerard chuckled. "Action-adventure, it is." He nodded toward the sofa. "Have a seat. What would you like to drink?"

"I can get it," she said. "You don't have to wait on me."

Gerard handed her the bowl of popcorn. "It's my pleasure. Just give me your order, and I'll be right back with it."

"I'd like a beer," Bernie said. "I'd go for whiskey, but I want to remain half-aware and fully awake for all the action scenes."

"Got it." Gerard tipped his head toward the kitchen. "I hope you don't mind that I made myself at home."

"Not at all," Bernie said. "Do you need help finding anything?" She started to follow him.

Gerard turned back. "Nope. I already found the popcorn and sodas. I saw beer in the fridge, cookies in the pantry and seasoning salt on the counter. What more do we need?"

Bernie grinned. "Sounds like you have it covered."

"Find a seat, choose your poison in your favorite action movie. I'll be right back."

Bernie smiled as she leaned back on the couch, glad Gerard was setting expectations of a calm night, watching a movie and eating popcorn. Nothing sexual about it. Just a bodyguard making sure his client was sufficiently entertained and distracted from the day's events.

She could handle that and keep calm, cool and collected, resisting the desire to touch the man and feel just how hard his muscles were.

Her fingers tightened on the popcorn bowl, reminding her to keep her hands to herself.

Bernie set the bowl aside and reached for the remote. As she scrolled through the movies offered, she finally selected an action-adventure with a broad brush of comedy, *Jumanji*, with Dwayne Johnson and Jack Black.

Gerard returned with two cans of beer and a package of cookies. He laid a can and the cookies on the coffee table. After he popped the top open on the other can, he handed it to Bernie.

"You can start without me. I want to shower before I sit on your sofa."

"Good idea," she said. "The hallway bathroom should have soap, shampoo and fresh towels. Yell, if you need anything else."

"Thanks," he said and disappeared down the hallway, carrying his backpack.

Bernie held the remote in her hand, fully intending to start the movie. Instead, she listened for sounds coming from the bathroom, her imagination going through the motions Gerard must be performing.

The sound of the shower running flooded Bernie's mind with images of Gerard. He'd be standing tall and naked beneath spray, water running over his head and shoulders, dripping down over his torso. As rivulets ran lower, they would slide over the jutting evidence of his desire.

The bathroom door opened before Bernie realized the water had long since stopped running.

Gerard stepped out, wearing only a pair of gym shorts, no shirt.

Bernie grabbed her beer, tipped the can back and took a long swallow, hoping the alcohol would take the edge off her anxiety. It helped…to an extent.

Gerard pulled a T-shirt over his head and settled on the cushion beside her. "You didn't start the movie."

She gave him a crooked smile. "Thinking."

"About?"

The way you make me feel.

Bernie stared at the television. "Everything that happened today."

"Hard not to, huh?" He started the movie, setting the volume low, and passed her the package of cookies.

Bernie sipped on her beer, hyper-aware of Gerard's thigh brushing against hers.

He leaned back and draped his arm over the back

of the couch, his fingertips brushing against her shoulder.

The television could burst into flames, and Bernie wouldn't notice. Her focus was homed in on the hand brushing against her shoulder and his thigh bumping into hers.

"Besides the resort trying to buy you out, do you have any other enemies who want to harm you?"

She shook her head. "Other than my father walking out on me and my mother when I was a baby, I've led a pretty normal, boring life."

"What about your husband? Did he have any enemies?"

"No," Bernie said. "His family has been a part of this community for decades."

"What about your father?" Gerard asked. "Does he keep in touch?"

Bernie shook her head. "I haven't heard from him, ever. He disappeared out of our lives, and I'm okay with that. The only good thing he did for me was provide the sperm to make me. From what I've learned over the years, he was the town bad boy from the wrong side of the tracks. My mother had the misfortune of falling in love with him. She spent the rest of her life paying for it."

"How so?"

"Being a single mother in a small town doesn't offer many options. She couldn't afford to go to college and had to work two jobs to keep a roof over our heads. She couldn't move out of town because she didn't have backup for childcare."

"That had to be hard for your mother," Gerard said softly.

"It was," Bernie said. "As an infant, I stayed with my grandparents. Once I started school, I'd get off the bus at their house. Only they were older, having had my mother later in life. My mother and I lived in a garage apartment for years until I was a teen and earning a little money of my own. I was able to buy my own clothes from a secondhand store in New Orleans, and I saved my summer work money for a car. It wasn't much of a car, and it drank oil, but it got me around to other jobs. We were able to move out of the garage apartment into a house we rented on the edge of town."

"You and your mother sound like fighters," Gerard said.

"We were," Bernie said. "Only there was one fight my mother didn't win." She swallowed hard on the lump in her throat. "A head-on collision with a drunk driver."

Gerard reached for her hand and curled his fingers around hers. "I'm sorry."

She shrugged, holding back her tears. "I was a senior in high school. She died a month before graduation. I promised myself I'd go to graduation for her."

"Did you?"

Bernie nodded. "I would not have graduated high school if not for my mother. I would not be alive today if not for my mother. I wouldn't be the person I am if not for her." A single tear slipped from the corner of her eye. "Like her, I'm not a quitter. She never quit. A drunk driver beat her, but she didn't go down without a fight."

"I think I would've liked your mother," Gerard said. "And maybe your father did you a favor by leaving."

Bernie had harbored so much anger toward her father for so many years. She'd watched her mother work herself into exhaustion just to make ends meet. Had he been there, he could have helped. At the very least, he could have paid child support to ease her burden. "It took me years to come to the same conclusion. He could've been an alcoholic, into drugs or a criminal. Mom and I were better off without that added nightmare."

Gerard stared for a long moment at the television as if he didn't see the people moving around on the screen.

Bernie wondered what he was thinking.

Then he turned to her with a tight smile. "And your grandparents?"

"When my mother died, I couldn't afford the rent on my own. I moved in with my grandparents, which worked out for them as they were at the point they needed help. My grandmother died of a stroke when I was a junior in college. My grandfather succumbed to dementia and had to enter a memory care facility the year I graduated college. He lived for another seven years." Her lips pressed together. "Everything he owned had to be sold to help pay for his care, including the house."

"I'm sorry. You must've loved them a lot to stay and help them through their final years."

"I did," she said. "They were good, loving people." She still missed them and her mother. She'd never really been alone until they'd all passed away.

"How did you meet your husband?"

She should have felt awkward talking about her husband while still holding Gerard's hand, but somehow, she didn't. He hadn't made a pass at her and wasn't flirting. He was being nice like a friend, making it easier for her to talk about Ray.

"I worked a couple of jobs in Bayou Mambaloa. I guess I was considering moving to New Orleans to make a better paycheck but hadn't committed. One of my jobs was for a local company designing ads and copy for businesses. Ray was one of our clients. He came by the office more often than necessary when I was designing the artwork and ad copy for Bellamy

Acres. I didn't realize at first that he was flirting with me. My boss had to point it out." Heat rose up into her cheeks. "I didn't date in high school. I was too busy making enough money to help with the rent and groceries. Sounds silly that I didn't know he was actually flirting."

"Not silly at all," Gerard said. "You're a beautiful woman."

Bernie snorted. "Hardly. But Ray thought I was pretty and smart. He said he'd seen me around town, helping other people, working hard, both physically and mentally. He admired my willingness to do whatever it took to make it in the world, much like him. On our first date, he took me out to his farm. It was his life, his heritage and his passion. I fell in love with his drive and determination to work the land his ancestors had cultivated."

"And you're carrying on his dream," Gerard said.

"Trying to," Bernie said.

"And doing a helluva a job." He gently squeezed her fingers. "Not only am I impressed, but the rest of my team is also."

Bernie leaned back against the couch cushion. "I'm sorry for monopolizing this conversation. I promise, I never talk this much." She turned toward him. "What about you? Where did you grow up? What was life like for young Gerard? Any siblings? I always wanted a brother or sister."

Gerard let go of her hand and reached for the popcorn bucket, a shadow descending across his face. "I grew up in Lafayette, Louisiana. And you were right. You were better off without your father. I wasn't as lucky. My father stayed."

Her chest squeezed hard at the tightness in his tone. Bernie reached out and laid a hand on his knee. "How bad was it?"

He stared down at her hand on his knee. "You don't want to hear this."

"Yes, I do," she said, her tone firm. "I want to know the man who's protecting me."

He looked at the television screen as he spoke quietly. "When he wasn't drinking, he was barely tolerable. But there weren't many days that he wasn't drinking. Mom took the brunt of his abuse, standing between him and me and my younger brother. Whenever I tried to stop him, he'd knock me across the room and go back to punching my mother."

Bernie couldn't imagine a young boy witnessing his father hitting his mother and not being able to stop him. He was right. It was better to be fatherless than to live in fear for yourself and someone you love.

"He swore I'd never amount to anything. He said I was stupid, like my mother." He shook his head. "I vowed that I would prove him wrong. As soon as I graduated high school, I joined the Marines and got the hell out of his house. I pushed myself hard to be the best in everything I did. When I applied for Marine Force Recon training, I was accepted and fought my way through . It wasn't as hard for me as some of the others. I never had it easy. My father made sure of that."

Bernie's heart hurt for Gerard. Growing up without a father didn't mean she'd grown up without love. Her mother had loved her with all her heart, and her grandparents had showered their only granddaughter with affection.

"I knew I could make it through the training if I just kept putting one foot in front of the other," Gerard said. "All the while, I saved every cent I made until I had enough to pay for a good lawyer and put a down payment on a house in Gulfport, Mississippi. I took two weeks' leave, showed up at my father's house in Lafayette, packed up my mother and brother and moved them to Gulfport."

Bernie's eyes widened. "Your father didn't try to stop you?"

Gerard's jaw hardened. "He tried."

Bernie sat up straight, her heart beating faster. "And?"

"Let's just say I let him have the first swing. I only hit him once. It surprised me how easily he went down. The man who'd seemed larger than life and could knock me across the room as a kid was a lightweight with a full-grown man." He drew in a breath and let it out slowly. "I told him if he ever bothered my mother or brother again, I wouldn't go as easy on him."

"How long has it been?" Bernie asked.

"Ten years."

"And your mother and brother?" she persisted.

"Mom got her divorce within a couple of months. She went to college and got a degree and now works as a counselor for victims of abuse."

Bernie's heart swelled. "Your brother?"

Gerard smiled. "Mason earned a college degree in engineering and joined the Army as a butter-bar, second lieutenant."

"What about you?" Bernie's voice softened. "I assume you're not married. Is that a valid assumption?"

He nodded.

"Were you ever?" She held her breath, wanting to know what kind of woman could have broken his heart.

"No." Gerard met her gaze. "I vowed never to marry."

Bernie blinked. "Why? You're nice-looking, strong and successful. Any woman would be happy to say I do."

His lips quirked for a second, then flatlined. "I'm the product of my mother and father. I have my father's genes as well as my mother's in me. I couldn't live with myself if I turned out to be an abuser like him."

"That's ridiculous. Have you ever hit a woman?" she asked.

He shook his head. "No. But I've never let one close long enough to get angry with her."

"You're not your father, Gerard. You proved that when you moved your mother out of his house and was restrained enough to hit him only once."

"I wanted to hit him again." Gerard's hands bunched into fists. "And I wanted to keep hitting him until his face was a bloody mess."

She touched his arm. "But you didn't. You have the control he lacked. You're not like him."

"I can't take that chance. I'd never forgive myself if I hurt a woman." He pushed to his feet and took several steps away, putting physical and emotional distance between them. "It's getting late, and we have a busy day tomorrow."

Bernie didn't press the issue. She knew in her heart Gerard was nothing like his father. The few short hours she'd known him had made it clear. He had a gruff exterior, but inside, he was kind, caring and capable of so much love.

He needed a special woman to bring him out of his shell.

In the very back of her mind, a voice whispered, *I wish it could be me.*

Ignoring the voice, she bid him good night. "The window air conditioner in the living room hasn't worked since last summer. I leave the bedroom door open to keep it cool in here."

"Do you know what's wrong with it?" he asked.

She nodded. "It's shot. I bought a new one but haven't had time to install it. One of these days, when I get the money, I want to put in a whole new air conditioning system. But that's way down the list of priorities. So, I apologize if it's too warm in here to sleep. I'll leave the bedroom door open, though."

"I've slept in worse places," he assured her.

"Well, then, good night." She strode for the master bedroom and paused in the doorway. "Thank you for being here for me. And, for the record, I don't think you could hurt a woman. You're not your father." Bernie dove through the door without waiting for his response.

In the dark, with only starlight shining through an open curtain to guide her, she crossed to the air conditioning window unit. After adjusting it to a cooler setting, she aimed the vents toward the open door, hoping it would help cool the living room for Gerard. The hum of the motor made it difficult for her to hear disturbances outside the house or even the sound of movement in the other room. No wonder someone had been able to lay Gertrude's body on her porch without her knowing. She'd brought Howey in for that night, and he'd slept on the floor at the foot of her bed.

Tonight, she'd made it a point to leave him outside. She might not hear someone placing a dead goose on her porch over the air conditioner's hum, but she'd hear the bay of her hound dog if anyone tried to get close to the house.

Bernie stood in the darkness, shimmied out of her bra and readjusted her T-shirt before lying across her bed on top of the sheets, too warm to slip beneath them. Her room was cool enough, but her blood ran hot through her veins.

A tall, handsome, intriguing man lay on the couch in the other room in a thin T-shirt and gym shorts.

Ray had been the same height as Bernie. She'd always felt on equal footing with him. Standing near Gerard made her tip her head back, leaving her feeling a little off-balance. Or was she off-balance because he made her pulse quicken and her breathing more labored?

Bernie lay staring up at the ceiling, wide awake and far too aware of the man in the other room. She'd loved her husband and grieved his loss, but she was still young enough to want a man's touch and the intimacy of lying naked, skin to skin.

Images of the day flooded her mind.

Gertrude's limp body on the porch.

A Marine showing up to help.

Penelope the pig running rampant in the watermelon patch.

The foot.

A ring.

Harvesting melons with a team of former military hunks.

A man sleeping in her house after three years of being on her own.

Her core aching with a need she'd long since set aside.

Moaning softly, she rolled onto her side and squeezed her eyes shut. She needed sleep, not sex.

CHAPTER 5

GERARD MADE a pass through the small farmhouse, checking door and window locks, making notes where some of the latches on the windows were loose and needed to be tightened the next day.

When he'd brought his backpack inside, he'd tucked his handgun inside. He took it out, checked that the magazine was fully loaded, the safety was on and laid it on the table beside the sofa.

As he stretched out on the sofa, his feet hung off the end. Not that he minded. It beat sleeping on the ground in a desert where you ate, drank and breathed sand in everything you did. So, what if the AC wasn't working in the living room? If he laid still enough, he could feel the cool air wafting through the open door of Bernie's bedroom.

His groin tightened at the thought of her lying on

ELLE JAMES

her bed, those long, bare legs moving between the sheets. In that moment, he could imagine what they'd feel like wrapped around his waist.

Immediately, his groin tightened, and his cock swelled. He swallowed hard to keep from groaning aloud.

Bernie was unlike any woman he'd ever met. She was certainly taller than most and not as classically beautiful as some, but she had a confidence and inner glow that shone through when she smiled.

And she'd done something no other woman he'd met had been able to do.

She'd made him want a different life than he'd mapped out for himself.

He'd researched what made a person abusive. So often, if a child was raised by an abusive parent, he became an abusive adult.

Watching his mother tremble, the fear in her eyes, the acceptance that she could do nothing to stop the beatings, had marked Gerard for life. He never wanted to see a woman cower in fear because of him. As angry as he'd been at his father, he could see how a man could lose control. He'd never forgive himself if he lost control and hit a woman.

So, he'd never let himself get too deeply into a relationship. After a date or two, he'd walked away.

Except now. Assigned to protect Bernie, he

106

couldn't walk away. Even if he could...he didn't want to.

The woman intrigued him. She made him want to spend more time with her. If it meant back-breaking work picking watermelons, he would do it.

Sitting beside her on the sofa, he'd fought the overwhelming urge to take her into his arms and kiss her. To hold her close and feel the warmth of her skin against his. As he lay on the same cushions where she'd been, he fantasized about stripping her naked and making love to her there in the living room.

His cock hardened, and his pulse raced.

Bernie was so close physically, just a few short steps away, but still so far out of his reach that he might as well cool it.

She wasn't the kind of female a man had a one-night-stand with. She was an until-death-do-us-part woman whom a man committed to.

Gerard wasn't the man for her. He might as well get the thought out of his head now. He was there to protect her. Nothing more.

He closed his eyes and willed sleep to come. It didn't. Several times over the next hour, he lit the dial on his watch. Time crawled. Would this night ever end?

A low woof sounded from the porch outside the front window.

Gerard sat up straight.

A bark, louder this time, was followed by what could only be described as a honking sound.

Gerard lunged to his feet, pulled on his boots and grabbed his gun.

He was heading for the door when footsteps sounded behind him.

A glance over his shoulder brought him up short.

Bernie rushed from her room, wearing shorts, dingo boots and a T-shirt, her nipples tight little points against the soft fabric. She carried a shotgun. "You heard that, right?"

He nodded. "You should stay inside. I can check it out."

"Like hell. Those are my animals. I won't let some bastard kill another one of them on my watch." She caught up with him as he reached the door.

Gerard's hand closed over the doorknob before Bernie could grab it. "At least let me go outside first," he insisted.

She hesitated in the soft light glowing from a nightlight near the front entrance. Her brow furrowed, but she gave him a curt nod. "Wait."

Gerard's hand froze on the knob.

Bernie reached around him, her breasts brushing against his arm, and lifted a flashlight from a mounted bracket beside the door. She handed it to him. "Take this."

He held the light in one hand and his pistol in the other.

Bernie grabbed a headlamp from a hook beside the wall bracket and slipped it over her head.

Gerard would rather have had night vision goggles, but a flashlight was better than nothing if he couldn't make out shapes in the starlight.

Gerard had his own handgun, but Hank Patterson had equipped each team member with a pair of night vision goggles, an armor-plated vest and a radio headset, all of which were in the boarding house, except the handgun he carried with him everywhere.

Without turning on the porch light, he slipped through the front door, down the steps and out into the yard.

The barking and honking had moved farther away from the house and seemed to be coming from the field past the barn.

Bernie ran down the steps. "That's Gandolf and Howey. Sounds like there's trouble in the water-melon patch."

Before he could stop her, she ran past him and around the side of the house.

He gave chase, quickly catching up and passing her, heading for the noise.

Once out in the open field, starlight gave them just enough light to make out a blur of white motion.

"There," Bernie pointed. "That's Gandolf. Howey will be close."

They picked their way through the vines until they reached the goose and hound dog.

Gandolf flapped his wings, honking loudly.

Grunting snorts filled the air.

Bernie swore. "What the hell?" She switched on her light and shined it around the watermelon patch.

Every one of the pigs that had been in the temporary corral was scattered across the section of the watermelon patch they'd already picked.

"They're heading for the unpicked melons," Bernie said. "We have to stop them before they get there."

"How?"

"I need you to head them off before they get there," Bernie said. "I'm going back to the barn for a bucket of grain."

Gerard didn't like the idea of Bernie going back alone, but the pigs had almost made it to the unpicked part of the patch.

"I'll be fine," she assured him as she spun and ran toward the barn.

Careful not to trip over vines and melons, Gerard worked his way over to the pigs and positioned himself between them and the melons that were ready to be picked the next day. Unsure of how he was supposed to keep a dozen pigs from marching right past him, he raised his arms and waved like Bernie had earlier with Penelope. "Go on," he said. "Back to your pen."

The pigs fell back a few steps, swung wide and made another attempt to enter the land of juicy melons.

"No way," Gerard said and hurried to head them off.

With every attempt, they moved a little closer.

Gerard flapped his arms and yelled at them, but they weren't scared or impressed. He couldn't let them get to the melons, but short of shooting them, there wasn't enough of him to keep all of them from getting where they wanted to go. Not to mention, some of them were twice his weight and could easily trample him to death.

He tried not to dwell on that thought.

Just when he thought the pigs would win the race, he heard the sound of grain being shaken in a tin pail.

"Here, pig," Bernie called out. She shook the pail as she neared the pigpen. "Here, pig."

The pigs that had been intent on reaching the ripe watermelons looked toward the sound of the grain in the bucket and Bernie's voice calling out to them.

She shook the bucket again. "Here, pig."

A large sow, Gerard guessed was Penelope, turned and trotted toward Bernie.

The others, curious, hurried to catch up, eager to get the grain Bernie offered.

Instead of herding them back into the makeshift pen of corral panels, Bernie opened the gate to their regular pen and dumped most of the grain from the bucket into a feed trough.

Gerard followed behind the herd, shining his flashlight into the shadows, searching for any strays that might not have been tempted by the grain.

When he reached the pen, his boots sank into the mud. While the majority of the field had dried during the day, the ground by the pen was still wet from the rain the night before. Bernie stood near the gate, a frown denting her brow. "I'm missing one."

Gerard attempted to turn, but the suction of the mud kept him in place.

"Oh, there he is," Bernie said. "Better move. He's coming in fast."

Gerard tried to pull his booted foot out of the mud, only succeeding in bringing up his foot. The boot remained.

Balancing on one leg, he was trying to fit his foot back in the sunken boot when Bernie cried out. "Look out!"

Unable to move out of the way, Gerard could only swing his body halfway around in time to see a giant hog barreling toward him.

At the last second, the hog darted to the right, but

his big body bumped Gerard, sending him flying backward.

He landed on his ass in the smelly quagmire, holding the handgun and flashlight above the mud.

Once the hog was inside the pen, Bernie swung the gate shut, secured it and moved toward Gerard. "Are you all right?"

He held up his hand. "Don't come closer. This stuff is like quicksand. Once you're in it, the suction won't let go."

Too late. Bernie had already placed one of her feet in the muck. When she tried to pull it out, her foot came out of the boot.

Gerard rocked to his feet and reached out to steady Bernie. He wasn't quite close enough to catch her as she teetered on one leg.

She swayed, seemed to get her balance and then fell to her hands and knees. "Blast it."

Giving up on his boots, Gerard tucked his handgun in one of his pockets and the flashlight in the other.

With his hands free, he tramped through the muck barefooted and helped Bernie to an upright position.

"Leave the boots," he said.

"I can't do that," she said. "They're my good mud boots."

"Yes, you can. I'm going to lift you," he said.

"Leave the boots. I'll retrieve them after I get you out of this mess."

He bent, scooped her up into his arms and carried her one trudging step at a time past the mud to a dry patch of ground, where he set her on her feet.

Back into the slew, he waded and shined his flashlight around until he found her boots. He worked at them until he freed them from the mud and carried them back to Bernie.

Once more, he waded back into the slew, found his boots, freed them and made his way out of the muck to where Bernie waited. Covered in mud from head to toe, she was a mess.

A very cute mess.

If not for the stench, he might have kissed her.

She stared at the corral panels in the starlight. One of the panels was lying on the ground. "I don't think the pigs knocked that panel down."

Gerard shined his flashlight at the portable fence panels. The metal clamps that had held them together lay on the ground nearby. "I don't know many pigs that can work a wrench or a screwdriver."

"Which means someone let them out. Like someone let Penelope out last night." Bernie turned toward the watermelon patch. "Why would someone let the pigs out?"

"Look what Penelope did in a few short hours," Gerard pointed out. "If Howey and Gandolf hadn't raised the alarm, just think what all those pigs would've done to the watermelons."

Bernie nodded. "I lost a lot just to Penelope. I rely on my crops to bring in enough money to cover my bills for the year. Without that money, I'd have to find a job. To find a job, I'd have to go to a city. I couldn't run Bellamy Acres. I couldn't take care of the animals. This place would fall into disrepair. I could lose it if I couldn't pay the taxes on it."

"Do you think someone is trying to sabotage you?"

She shrugged. "Maybe. If someone is just pranking me...I'm not laughing."

"Come on," he said. "It might take a dozen showers and strong soap to get the smell out by morning."

"No kidding." Bernie stared at him in the light from the stars overhead. "Wow. Do I look as bad as you?"

"You have one bare spot free of mud." His lips twitched as he reached out to touch a finger to the tip of her nose, leaving a smudge of mud. "There. Got you covered."

She laughed and then coughed. "The sooner we get back to the house, the sooner we can rinse this nastiness off."

"I don't know why you're in such a hurry." He

offered her his arm. "People pay for mud masks, don't they?"

Bernie laughed and slipped her hand through the crook of his elbow. "I'm willing to bet they don't smell like this."

As Gerard walked with Bernie back to the house, he fought to focus on the pigs, not how sexy she was when she laughed—even covered in muck.

"We'll have to hose off and strip before we go into the house," Bernie said. "If we don't, we bring that stench with us."

"Agreed," Gerard said, though he only heard the part about stripping.

Bernie led him to the side of the house and stopped in front of a spigot with a hose attached. She dropped her boots on the ground, turned on the water and sprayed the boots until all the muck had been washed away. She handed the hose to Gerard and then set her boots on the porch to dry.

Gerard sprayed his boots to remove all the mud and set them on the porch beside Bernie's.

"I can hold the sprayer over you while you rinse off," Gerard offered. "I promise to close my eyes."

Bernie didn't hesitate for long before she nodded. "Okay. But no peeking."

Gerard raised the sprayer over her head, closed his eyes and pressed the button to release a steady stream of water.

Through his eyelashes, he watched as Bernie rubbed her hands over her shirt and shorts, removing as much of the mud as possible. Once her T-shirt was soaking wet, it did little to hide her figure beneath. The fabric clung to the swell of her breasts, and her nipples were pointy nubs, tempting Gerard to take them.

Bernie shoved her shorts down over her hips and stepped out of them. The shirt was next. She turned her back to him, grabbed the hem, tugged the T-shirt over her head and hung it on the porch rail.

Since her back was to him, Gerard didn't bother to keep his eyes closed. His gaze swept her from the top of her head to the backs of her heels, slowly devouring the curve of her waist and the luscious swell of her hips and buttocks.

The steady spray had washed away the mud from her skin, leaving it shiny and wet. Starlight reflected off the droplets, making her appear ethereal in the darkness.

When she glanced over her shoulder, he quickly closed his eyes.

"I'm headed for the shower," she said. "I promise to save you some hot water."

"You don't have to. Soap and a cold shower will be sufficient for me," he said. And necessary. He was glad for the darkness, hoping it was enough to hide his arousal.

Naked and clean of the mud, she darted for the steps. "Leave the clothes on the ground," she called over her bare shoulder. "I'll collect them tomorrow morning."

Starlight bathed her pale body in indigo as she hurried up the steps. As she pulled the door open, she turned just enough to expose the side of a full breast.

Sweet Jesus, she was beautiful.

"You weren't supposed to peek," she said.

"Sorry, I thought you were already inside," he lied, unable to tear his eyes from her svelte form.

She chuckled, her lips curving in a smile. "Liar." Bernie started to go into the house, paused and turned enough to tease him with that breast again. "Just so you know...the shower in the master bathroom is big enough for two." She lifted her chin. "I'm not opposed to sharing. You're call."

Bernie disappeared into the house, her words hanging in the air like a red cape dangled in front of a raging bull.

CHAPTER 6

GERARD KNEW what he *should* do.

He should rinse off, wait his turn for a shower, clean up and sleep.

Alone.

But Bernie had thrown out an invitation...a challenge.

"Challenge accepted," he murmured, adrenaline pulsing through his veins. He quickly rinsed his clothes, stripped them from his body and rinsed the mud from his skin. He couldn't go fast enough. In the back of his mind, he was afraid he was taking too long, giving Bernie enough time to change her mind and regret her invitation.

After he turned off the spigot and shook off the excess water, he jogged toward the stairs and took them two at a time. At the top, Howey the hound dog sat on his haunches beside the door as a reminder that he was on guard duty.

Gerard scratched behind the animal's ear. "Good boy."

Howey's tail thumped against the porch planks.

Gerard grinned, grateful for what he interpreted as Howey's approval, and stepped across the threshold into the house. He turned and locked the door behind him. Barefoot and dripping, he strode through the living room, entered the bedroom and stopped at the open bathroom door.

The shower was running, steam clouding the glass enclosure.

Gerard reminded himself that Bernie was his client. A woman who believed in commitment and deserved a man who would love, honor and cherish her until death.

He, on the other hand, couldn't commit, afraid his father's genes would eventually emerge. He almost turned and walked away.

Bernie's silhouetted figure appeared through the foggy glass, hazy and sexy as hell.

Gerard couldn't walk away.

The shower door opened, and Bernie poked her head out, her face, neck and shoulders glistening with moisture. When she spotted him, she opened the door wider and held out her hand.

Against his better judgment, Gerard took her

hand and stepped into the shower. "We shouldn't," he murmured.

"You're right," she said with a smile and handed him a bottle of body wash. "We shouldn't miss this opportunity. I'll do you if you'll do me."

Gerard groaned. "I don't have protection."

She reached behind her to the soap tray and raised a packet. "Gotcha covered. And I'm not asking for forever. I'll settle for tonight, no strings, no regrets." She raised an eyebrow. "Any more concerns?"

His lips spread into a grin. "None." He squirted soap into his palm, set the bottle down and rubbed the liquid between his hands until he had a sudsy lather.

Bernie took his hands in hers and guided them to her breasts. As she laid his hands on her skin, she drew in a deep breath, and the rounded globes filled his palms.

He groaned and moved his hands, pinching the tips of her nipples between his thumbs and fore-fingers.

Bernie tilted her head back and let the shower's spray wash over her chest and torso. "Mmm. More, please." She wrapped her calf around the back of his leg, drawing him closer so that her sex pressed against his thigh. She rode it, rubbing her pussy against his coarse hairs.

Gerard cupped her breasts fully in his hands and squeezed gently. Eventually, he abandoned them to slide his hands over her ribs and downward to the juncture of her thighs.

She eased back, allowing his hand to slide between her legs.

He lowered his head and kissed her as his fingers slipped between her folds and strummed her clit.

Bernie leaned back against the cool tiles of the shower and spread her legs wider, giving him the room he needed to please her.

And please her he did, flicking that nubbin of nerves until she bucked against his hand.

Gerard would have taken her against the wall, but he wouldn't until she came first. He needed to move the magic into the bedroom, where he could focus on her.

"Let's finish up here," he suggested and poured more soap on his hand.

Bernie frowned. "Are we done?"

He laughed. "Not even close to done." Gerard rubbed soap all over her body, shampooed her hair and swept his fingers over every inch of her.

Bernie returned the favor, her hands gliding across his chest and downward to capture his erection in a firm grip.

Her strong yet supple fingers caressed him, sliding up and down his length.

With each pass, Gerard's cock swelled, growing harder by the second. When he teetered on the verge of release, he captured her hands. "Not yet."

He clutched her bottom and lifted.

Bernie's legs wrapped around his waist, her sex pressing down on his cock.

"Hold that thought," Gerard said through clenched teeth.

He set her on her feet outside the shower walls, turned off the water and grabbed a towel.

They made quick work of drying each other off. Although they were still damp in places, Gerard didn't care. He gathered Bernie in his arms, snagged the condom from the soap dish and carried her into the bedroom, laying her on the bed.

Gerard straightened, feasting his gaze on her naked body.

She touched her breast with one hand and reached out to clasp his dick in the other. "Make love to me."

He drew in a breath and let it out, his hold on control slipping with each stroke of her hand. Blood flowed hot and thick through his veins, heading south to his cock. If he didn't stop her soon, he'd come.

Gerard removed her fingers from around his erection, shaking his head. "I want this to last more than a few seconds. What you're making me feel...I want you to feel before I take you."

Her lips stretched in a wicked grin. "Then I'm doing it right. For a moment, I thought you didn't like it."

"Oh, I like it, all right. Too much." He climbed onto the bed beside her and trailed a finger across her cheek to her lips. "I want you to come first." He leaned over and captured her mouth beneath his, claiming her lips, then sweeping inside to caress her tongue.

Bernie slid her hand behind the back of his neck and held him close.

The kiss was just the beginning of his campaign to make her lose control. After thoroughly exploring her mouth, he brushed his lips across her chin and down the length of her throat to where the pulse beat wildly at the base, matching the rhythm of his thundering heart.

Moving lower, he captured one of her breasts in his palm and the other in his mouth. He sucked gently and then flicked the beaded nipple until her back arched, pushing that breast deeper into his mouth.

Bernie moaned and wove her fingers into his hair, urging him to take his mouth lower.

He obliged, skimming his lips over her ribs and pausing to dip his tongue into her bellybutton. As he smoothed his hand along the curve of her waist and over the swell of her hip, he reveled in her silky-soft skin. The tension inside him spiked when he cupped her sex and dipped a finger into her slick channel.

So wet. For him. He could already imagine how good it would feel to slide inside her and have her channel contract around him.

Patience, he coached himself. He wanted her to want him as badly as he wanted her.

Slipping lower between her legs, he parted her folds with his thumbs and flicked her clit with the tip of his tongue.

Bernie gasped, and her hips rose off the mattress.

He chuckled. "Like that?"

"Yes," she said, her voice rushed, her chest rising and falling with erratic breaths. "Again!"

He flicked his tongue across her clit again.

Bernie's body tightened.

She was close.

Gerard swirled his tongue around and around that nubbin of nerves.

Bernie raised her knees, planted her heels in the mattress and then rocked her hips in rhythm to his strokes. When she froze in mid-rock, he didn't stop but kept going until her fingers dug into his scalp, and she cried out his name, "Gerard! Sweet Jesus."

For a long moment, her body pulsed, her fingers contracting and releasing in his hair.

Her bottom sank back to the mattress. "That was...that was..." She breathed in and out. "So good." Her hands slid over his shoulders, gripped his arms and dragged him up her body. "Tell me that was just the beginning."

"It's your call," he said as he leaned over her, his cock poised at her entrance.

"I want more."

He grinned. "Of the same?"

She shook her head. "You. Inside me. Now."

He chuckled, bent and kissed her long and hard while reaching for the foil packet he'd tossed onto the bed beside her. Gerard sat back on his heels, tore open the packet and rolled the condom over his engorged erection. Once more, he leaned over her and kissed her gently as he entered her.

Moving slowly, he pushed deeper, not wanting to hurt her by going too fast.

"Too slow," Bernie gasped. She reached for his buttocks, dug her fingers into his flesh and pulled him closer, sinking him deeper inside her.

When he was fully sheathed, he held steady, allowing her to adjust to him. Then he pulled out and slid back in, settling into a smooth rhythm.

With a tenuous hold on his control, he thrust into her again and again, trying to make it last as long as he could. When he shot over the edge, he buried himself deep inside her.

Her channel contracted around his pulsing shaft. He rode the wave of sensations all the way to the end. When he could breathe again, he collapsed on top of her and rolled their bodies onto their sides, maintaining their intimate connection.

Bernie smoothed her hand over his naked back and down to cup his ass. "You're still so hard."

"And will be for a while."

She planted her hands on his chest and pushed him over onto his back, going with him until she was lying on top of him, straddling his hips.

"My turn." Bernie rose on her knees then came down on his rod. Inhaling deeply, her chest rose and fell, and a smile spread across her face. "I didn't want to waste a good hard-on when I could do this."

She rocked up and down for several more minutes, her breasts bouncing with her movements.

Gerard reached out, cupped her breasts, and squeezed softly. "You're so beautiful."

She shook her head without breaking her rhythm. "There are a lot prettier women than me."

"You underestimate yourself. When you smile, your face glows and makes me want to smile." His lips twisted. "Some of the members of my team would call that a miracle."

"You do have an intensity about your face." She leaned over to cup his cheek in her palm. "I find it intriguing." Bernie brushed her lips across his, her breasts pressing into his chest.

"Definitely beautiful," he whispered into her mouth.

"Shut up and kiss me," she said.

He wrapped his arms around her and returned her kiss, loving that she'd initiated it and wanted to keep going after he'd climaxed.

Soon, her movements slowed, and she laid down on him, resting her cheek against the curve of his neck. "I don't want this night to end," she whispered.

Neither did Gerard.

This woman was an accomplished farmer, capable of caring for her menagerie of animals, planting fields of produce and harvesting the fruits of her labors. She was also an amazing lover with strong legs, smooth skin and luscious breasts. If he wasn't careful, he'd fall in love with her.

That was something he couldn't do.

Bernie deserved a good man. A man who would never hurt her. A gentle man who would treat her kindly and love her forever.

Gerard wished he could be that man. But he was afraid that he would snap and unleash the beast inside him under pressure. He could become a monster just like his father.

Unwilling to risk that, he realized that night would be the only one he could share with this amazing woman. Tomorrow, he'd focus on the job and put distance between himself and Bernie, if not physically, then mentally. She was his client and could never be anything more.

A deep ache grew in his chest. Walking away from other women hadn't bothered him.

This time would be different.

Bernie's breathing deepened, and her body went limp on him.

When he rolled her onto her side, she snuggled against him, laying an arm over his chest and a leg over his thigh.

Gerard held her well into the early hours of the morning. Like Bernie had said, he didn't want the night to end. He could get used to sleeping with this woman at his side, her supple body pressed against his.

BERNIE HADN'T EXPECTED to sleep after all that had happened the day before. She was surprised when the alarm went off, signaling it was time to get up and move. They had a load of watermelons to deliver and more to pick.

She stretched, her arm colliding with a solid wall of muscle. A rush of heat spread through her body and coiled at her core.

"Morning, beautiful," Gerard said, his voice gravelly from sleep.

"Already?" Bernie slid her hand over his chest and down to where his cock jutted straight up, tenting the sheet. "Mmm. One of the benefits of being male. I think we can spare a few minutes."

She curled her hand around his shaft and slid it up and then downward to roll his balls between her fingers.

He captured her hand with his. "We shouldn't do this," he said.

"Too late," Bernie smiled. "We already have. And you can't take it back."

"But we don't have to continue doing it," he pointed out.

Her hand stilled halfway up his cock. "Tell me you don't want this, and I'll stop."

"I don't..." He paused. "Oh, who am I kidding? I want you more than I want to breathe." With a sigh, he closed his hand around hers. "I don't want you to stop."

"Good, because I wasn't sure I could stop for long. I'm so hot and horny, if you didn't help me out, I'd have to dig out my vibrator."

"Mmm." He pressed his lips to the spot just below her earlobe. "That would be interesting." His hand slipped between her legs, and he stroked her clit until she was squirming against the mattress, her desire pushing her past horny to full-on orgasm in record time.

He played her clit until the tingling subsided, but she wanted more of him.

Gerard flung back the sheet, turned Bernie onto her belly and lifted her hips until she came up on her knees.

With her bare ass in the air and her elbows resting on the bed, she was exposed to Gerard and so turned on she could hardly wait for him to thrust into her.

Making love with Ray had been confined to two positions. Him on top or her on top. He'd never come from behind or taken her on the kitchen table or in the barn.

This was new to her and exciting.

Gerard gripped her hips, pulled her close and slipped his cock between her legs. He missed her entrance but rubbed against her clit, making her jerk with titillating awareness.

Bending over her, he stroked her clit with his finger while sliding his shaft past her pussy, grazing it each time.

Bernie creamed, the juices coating his cock with each passing.

About the time the teasing turned to frustration, Gerard pressed his member against her entrance and stopped. "Protection."

"In the nightstand," she said between gritted teeth, her entire body poised on the edge of an epic orgasm.

Gerard reached into the top drawer, found a packet, tore it open and rolled it down over his cock. Then he was back, his dick pressing into her slick channel. He took her all the way in a smooth, easy stroke.

His hands on her hips held her steady while he pumped in and out of her.

She leaned back into him, her back arching, her head thrown back. The tension inside built until her muscles and nerves were stretched so tightly that all it would take to send her over the edge was...

With his cock filling her inside, he flicked her clit with the tip of his finger.

Bernie burst over the edge, her heart racing, her breathing straining to keep up. Tingling began from her core and spread throughout her body. For a long moment, she remained where she was, milking the ecstasy to the very end. She sank to her belly on the mattress and lay there, filling her lungs with air.

When Gerard made no move to join her, Bernie flipped onto her back and stared up at him, where he still knelt on his knees.

"Are you all right?" she asked.

He nodded. "More than anything, I want to lay down beside you."

"Then do it," she urged.

He shook his head. "Duty's calling. We have to get those melons to New Orleans this morning. Bellamy Acres depends on it."

"Fuck duty." Bernie drank in Gerard's incredible body and then closed her eyes. "You're right." She opened her eyes. "When you own a farm, the farm owns you." She reached out. "Help me up."

He gripped her hand.

Instead of pulling herself up, she pulled him down until he lay on top of her.

"The melons can wait a few more minutes, don't you think?" She cupped his cheek and leaned up to brush her lips across his. "Unless you've had enough."

"I have a feeling there's no such thing as *enough* with you," he whispered against her lips and then claimed her mouth in a deep kiss that branded Bernie's soul.

God help her. She was falling fast.

CHAPTER 7

SLEEPING with a man changed everything in a relationship.

Gerard seemed closer yet more distant than before they'd made love. It was as if he struggled with what he wanted and what he couldn't have. Because of what his father had done to him and his mother, he didn't trust himself to always do the right thing. He'd chosen to walk away from love rather than end up hurting those he cared about. He'd push her away like he probably had every other woman he'd ever dated.

All Bernie knew was that this man was worth fighting for. She didn't need weeks of dating to figure that out. Despite his upbringing, or maybe because of it, he was a good man who cared about people and didn't want to hurt them. He didn't want to hurt her.

Thus, the wall he was attempting to construct between them.

What he didn't realize about her was that because she'd loved and lost, she was acutely aware that life was incredibly short. Shorter for some than others. She had to grab for happiness and hold on for as long as she could.

Though they were just beginning to know each other, Bernie knew in her heart this man was special. She didn't want what they'd shared the night before and this morning to end.

She just had to convince him to stay.

However, first, they had a delivery to make. She needed the money from her watermelon sales to pay her property taxes, which were due in a couple of weeks.

After a few minutes more of snuggling, Gerard kissed her temple. "You're thinking about the day ahead, aren't you?"

She sighed. "Hard not to. So much depends on getting my melons to market."

He kissed her temple again and rolled out of the bed. "Come on. We have a delivery to make, and we're burning daylight." He held out his hand.

She laughed, letting him pull her to her feet and into his arms. His naked skin against hers was amazing and far too tempting. Bernie slid her hands down his back to his bare ass and moaned. "Promise me we'll make time for this later tonight."

He hesitated a moment.

She thought he might say no, falling back on his vow to walk away from any commitment.

Bernie held her breath, waiting for him to say no.

"I promise," he said and hugged her close.

She released the breath she'd been holding and hugged him back.

"I'll make coffee while you get dressed."

"Deal." Bernie grabbed a bra and panties and ducked into the bathroom, closing the door behind her. For a moment, she leaned her back against the wall and smiled. After three long years alone, she'd slept with a man.

In the last few weeks of Ray's life, they'd talked about what she should do after he was gone. He'd given her permission to sell the place and move on.

"You're still young. There's no reason you can't fall in love with someone who can give you the children we wanted." He'd held her hand in his, his grip weak, his skin stretched thin over his bones.

Tears had slipped down her cheeks. "I don't know, Ray. That was *our* dream. I love *you*. I wanted children with *you*."

He'd given her a tight smile. "And I wanted them with you. But that's not how this story ends. I'll be gone. You have to keep living. There's someone special out there for you. He'll love, protect and care for you. And he'll give you babies to love. You always wanted a house full of kids. Don't give up on that dream. You'll make a terrific mother." He squeezed her hand with a surprising strength. "Promise me you'll give yourself the chance."

He wouldn't calm down and sleep until she'd made that promise. At the time, she'd had no intention of keeping it.

In the past three years, she'd worked so hard she hadn't had time to date, nor had she wanted to. No man had pushed past the grief of her loss or awakened her desire.

Until Gerard.

There's someone special out there for you.

Ray's prediction echoed in her memory.

Gerard was special. He could be the one. Only he would be a work in progress to get past his own baggage instilled by an abusive father.

Bernie pushed away from the wall, stepped into a cool shower and quickly rinsed off. After she dried herself with a towel, she pulled on the panties and bra. She stared at her reflection in the mirror and winced. How had she attracted a man looking like something the cat had dragged in?

Quickly running a brush through her hair, she worked out the tangles, pulled it back and braided it into a thick plait that hung down the middle of her back.

Ray had loved her hair long. It was even longer than when he'd died, but only because she hadn't taken the time to get it cut.

For a moment, she considered applying a little blush and mascara but ended up leaving the bathroom with her face bare. They'd be working in the field later. Any makeup would end up running down her face in sweat.

She left the bathroom, found a pair of jeans in her closet, pulled them up over her hips, and then found a clean, heather-gray T-shirt. She was a farmer, not a fashion model. After slipping into socks and her dingo boots, she made her way into the kitchen, following the rich aroma of coffee.

Gerard, fully dressed in jeans, a black T-shirt and tennis shoes, handed her a travel mug full of steaming brew. "I didn't know what you wanted in it. It's black."

"Perfect," she said and sipped, careful not to burn her tongue. "I can whip up some eggs and bacon if you'd like."

He nodded toward the counter, where a stack of toast lay on a paper towel. "I'm okay with toast if you'd like to hit the road as soon as possible."

She nodded. "Sounds good." She wrapped the

toast in the paper towel and headed for the door, snagging her purse off a hook on the wall.

Once outside, she glanced right and then left at the porch. "That's odd."

"What's odd?" he asked.

"Howey is usually asleep on the porch at this time."

Gerard grinned. "Isn't he usually asleep on the porch at all times, except when he's guarding the watermelon patch from intruders?"

Bernie descended the steps, careful not to spill her coffee. "Exactly." She glanced around the yard and looked toward the barn. "Howey!"

The dog didn't respond.

She ducked and looked beneath the porch. "Sometimes, he likes to sleep beneath the porch. He hides all his treasures beneath the steps. I have to clean it out every so often when he drags a dead animal under there." She frowned. "Howey?"

The dog didn't come out. She straightened. "He came back from the watermelon patch last night, didn't he?"

Gerard nodded, descending the stairs to stand beside Bernie. "I scratched behind his ear before I entered the house last night. He was sitting there by the door."

"Maybe he's out looking for more treasures,"

Bernie said with a smile. "He'll show up soon enough."

She led the way to where they'd left the truck hooked to the trailer with its huge cardboard boxes filled with watermelons.

Bernie double-checked that the hitch was safely connected and the lights and brakes were plugged securely into the back of the truck. When she turned to look at the boxes on the trailer, her brow dipped low. The bottom of the cardboard boxes were dark, as if they'd somehow gotten wet. Her heart skipped a beat. They'd been careful to pick them when they were dry and had loaded them carefully into the containers. A sense of dread crushed her chest as she climbed over the rail into the trailer and peered down into one of the boxes. "Son of a bitch."

"What?" Gerard asked.

"No, no, no." This could not be happening. Bernie moved to the next box and repeated, "Son of a bitch."

As Bernie continued to the next box, Gerard leaped onto the trailer and looked down into the cardboard container to see what she had seen.

The watermelons they'd stacked so carefully had been smashed into a wet, terrible mess.

"Are they all like this?" he asked.

Bernie glanced up for the last box, her face pale, her mouth pressed into a thin line. "All of them." She shook her head. "I don't understand. Who would do such a thing? And how did we not hear it happening?"

They had been in the shower and then the bedroom, where the air conditioning unit had been humming enough to mask the sound of someone smashing watermelons. But not loud enough she couldn't hear a dog bark. Her eyes widened. "Howey."

She jumped down from the trailer and ran around the front of the truck. "Check around the house," she commanded. "I'll look around the barn."

Gerard ran for the house while Bernie made a circle around the exterior of the barn.

Gerard arrived back from his perusal, shaking his head. "I didn't see him."

Bernie opened the small barn door beside the larger double doors, which were only used when driving big equipment in and out or bringing horses into stalls. As she stepped inside, she reached to switch on the light and almost tripped over a lump on the floor.

As the lights blinked on, Bernie realized the lump on the floor was Howey.

"Oh, dear God," she said and dropped to her knees beside him.

Gerard eased past her and the dog and knelt on the dirt floor. "Is he alive?"

Bernie laid her ear against the dog's chest and listened for a long moment, desperate to hear the beat of his heart or feel the rise and fall of the animal's chest as it filled with air.

She'd almost given up hope when she detected the faint rhythm of a pulse. "I hear a heartbeat," she said, her voice catching in her throat. She leaned back and checked the animal all over, lifting his paw to test for resistance but finding none. "I don't see any injuries. What's wrong with him? Why isn't he moving?"

"We need to get him to a vet," Gerard scooped his hands beneath Howey and lifted him.

"We'll take the produce truck. I don't have to unhitch it from a trailer. Go. I'll be right there."

Gerard carried Howey out of the barn.

Bernie ducked into a small office, snagged the spare keys for the produce truck and ran to get in front of Gerard. She opened the passenger door and waited for Gerard to climb in with Howey and settle into the passenger seat. Once they were in, she shut the door, ran around to the driver's side, climbed in and twisted the key in the ignition.

The engine turned over once and died.

"Come on," she urged and turned the key again. This time, the engine caught and roared to life.

With her foot on the clutch, she shifted into first, released the clutch and eased her foot onto the accelerator. The truck lurched forward, steadied and rumbled down the driveway as she headed for town.

She shot glances toward Gerard and Howey several times on the way. "Is he breathing?"

"I can't tell. But his body is still warm," Gerard replied, holding the dog close.

Bernie didn't slow much once she reached the outskirts of town. Dr. Saulnier, the only veterinarian in town, was two blocks past Broussard's Country Store and one block north of Main Street.

Bernie blew past the sheriff's office, the fire station and Broussard's, slowing as she neared the turn off Main. She took the turn a little faster than the old truck liked, the tires squealing as it slid sideways. Quickly straightening the wheels, she skidded to a stop in front of the vet's clinic.

The engine hadn't completely shut down by the time Bernie leaped from the driver's seat and rounded the hood to the passenger side.

She flung open the door and helped Gerard slide out with Howey. Once they were on the ground, Bernie ran ahead, opened the door to the clinic and waited for Gerard to enter. Then she was at the desk. "Linda, please tell me Dr. Saulnier is in. Something's wrong with Howey. I think someone tried to kill him."

Linda's eyebrows rose. "Oh, dear. Yes, the doctor is in. He's with a patient. I'll let him know it's an emergency." She rushed from the room into the back of the office. When she returned, Dr. Saulnier was with her.

"Bring him into exam room one," he said and led the way.

Once in the small room, the doctor had Gerard lay the dog on the stainless-steel table and immediately pressed his stethoscope to Howey's chest. "He has a heartbeat. It's slow but steady. Did he eat something he shouldn't have?"

"Not that I know of," Bernie said. "I think someone might have poisoned him. I found him in the barn with the door closed after I'd left him on the porch last night. And my trailer full of watermelons was destroyed. Howey always warns me when intruders are near the house or barn at night. Whoever smashed my melons had to have given him something to keep him quiet, or I would have heard him."

"Leave Howey with me," the doctor said. "I'll give him something to counteract poison and keep him under observation overnight. I'll keep you informed of his condition."

Bernie didn't want to leave Howey. What if he woke up and was confused about his surroundings? He'd think she'd abandoned him.

"As out of it as he is, it will be a while before he's coherent enough to care about his surroundings.

We'll take good care of him," Dr. Saulnier said. "Now, go. The sheriff needs to know what happened."

"He's right," Gerard cupped her elbow in his palm. "We need to let the sheriff know what happened."

She knew he was right, but she hated leaving Howey in a strange place with no one he knew to wake up to.

Bernie let Gerard guide her out of the office and into the parking lot. A sheriff's vehicle had pulled up behind the old produce truck, and Deputy Taylor was getting out.

"Bernie, what's going on?" she asked. "You blew through town like the devil was on your tail."

"It's Howey," Bernie said, choking on the lump rising in her throat. "He might d-die."

Taylor reached out and touched Bernie's arm. "Holy shit. What happened?"

"I—we—" Bernie started shaking and couldn't stop. She'd held it together for so long, staying strong for Ray throughout his battle with ALS, his death, the struggle to get the farm back up and running and now this.

Gerard folded her into his arms. "We need to get some food in you," he said.

"Take her to Tante Mimi's Diner," Deputy Taylor said. "I'll contact the sheriff, and we'll meet you there."

Gerard helped Bernie into the passenger seat of the old truck.

"I can drive," she said as he leaned across her to snap the belt into the buckle.

As he backed out, he brushed a kiss across her forehead. "I know you can, but let me help."

She didn't argue, glad for once that someone else was taking charge. As she sat back against the seat and stared ahead, a thousand thoughts came rushing at her like a firehose out of control. She couldn't process any of them, knowing Howey, her trusted hound dog, lay unconscious on a cold stainless-steel table because someone had likely poisoned him.

Gerard climbed into the driver's seat and secured his seatbelt. He turned to her. "Howey's in good hands. Dr. Saulnier will do everything he can to save him."

She knew he would, but what if he couldn't save him? Her heart lurched in her chest, and a tear rolled down her cheek. "Ray brought Howey home the day after the doctor told him the ALS had progressed, and there wasn't anything they could do." She swiped at the second tear. "He was just a puppy with big feet and big ears. All I could think when he carried him through the door was how much work he'd be while I was taking care of Ray through the end of his life."

Gerard reached out and wrapped his fingers around hers. He didn't speak, just listened.

"Ray said Howey would be the last puppy he would ever get to love. He said that Howey would be there for me when he was gone. Ray knew I needed to be needed. Before I'd met him, I'd lost everyone I'd ever loved. Losing him would leave me alone again. He couldn't stand the thought of me being alone." Tears spilled down her cheeks. She couldn't stop them. "If I lose Howey..."

Gerard's fingers tightened around hers. "It would be like losing Ray all over again."

She nodded.

"You loved him."

Again, she nodded.

"He was a lucky man," Gerard said softly.

She laughed. "Lucky? He died of ALS before he turned forty. How is that lucky?"

"He didn't die alone," Gerard said. "He had you. Your husband died knowing he was greatly loved. Not everyone is that fortunate."

"Howey can't die." Bernie blinked back tears, her jaw hardening. "He deserves to live a long, healthy life. Whoever did this to him...whoever killed Gertrude..." She couldn't think of any punishment painful enough to equal the pain she felt for her beloved pets. "This has to stop," she said, bunching her free hand into a fist. "Maybe I need to sell the farm and move my animals somewhere they won't be targeted by greedy investors."

"Your life might be easier if you didn't have to run a farm all by yourself," he said, "but is that what you really want?"

"No," she said. "I want whoever is targeting my farm and my animals to stop. I guess I need to stay awake all night to guard my animals and produce."

"That's not practical," Gerard said.

"I might as well." She waved her free hand. "I won't be able to sleep knowing someone might be out there hurting my animals and destroying my livelihood. As it is, I'll only make half what I had hoped to make on my melons, and only if I can deliver the other half intact. I was counting on that income to pay my taxes."

"We'll think of something," Gerard said.

"What? I can't grow a field of watermelons overnight. The season is ending. I won't be able to plant again until next spring. It'll be next fall before I can harvest again."

Gerard's hold on her hand tightened. "We'll figure it out." Then he let go and turned the key in the ignition. The engine started right up.

Of course, it did.

Bernie shook her head. She couldn't let this get to her. Nothing got better from whining about it.

She sat still while Gerard pulled out of the parking lot, drove onto Main Street and turned toward Tante Mimi's Diner.

"I'm sorry," Bernie said. "I'm not usually so negative."

"You're allowed to vent." He shot her a quick glance and returned his attention to the road. "It's been a shitty twenty-four hours."

"Not all of it," she said softly.

He looked again, his gaze gentle. "No, it hasn't all been so bad."

"No, it hasn't." She looked out the side window. "But the bad sure does suck."

"But knowing you now for a whole twenty-four hours, I know you won't give up. You're one of those that when the going gets tough..."

"—the tough get going," she finished, squaring her shoulders. She looked forward, her eyes narrowing. "I'm not a quitter. And they're not going to beat me. If they want a fight...bring it."

"That's my girl," Gerard said with a grin. "Let's get some food in you, talk to the sheriff and get back out to the farm to see what we can salvage."

Bernie was fired up and mad, ready to take on these people who were making her life hell. She only wished she knew who was doing it. She had an idea of who might be behind it, but the actual culprits? Not a clue.

If she had to, she'd sit up all night with her shotgun ready. When he showed up to commit more mayhem in an effort to scare her off her property, she'd fill the bastard's ass full of buckshot.

She'd teach him what happens when you kill a girl's goose and poison her dog.

CHAPTER 8

AT TANTE MIMI'S DINER, Mimi herself escorted Bernie and Gerard to a table. "I heard what happened to Howey," she said. "Sit down. I'll bring you some water, coffee, orange juice and cook anything you want, on the menu or not. On the house."

Bernie hugged Mimi. "You don't have to go to all that trouble. I doubt I could eat a bite."

Mimi held Bernie at arm's length. "You have to believe Howey will be all right. Think positive."

Bernie nodded. "You're right. He could use all the positivity he can get."

"Right." Mimi smoothed her hands over her apron. "What can I get you two to eat?"

Bernie shrugged. "Anything. Surprise me."

Mimi turned to Gerard. "And you?"

"Make it two," he said.

"Gotcha. I'll be right back." The woman spun, and her long black hair, encased in a hairnet, bobbed as she hurried toward a coffee pot behind the counter.

Gerard had been to the diner on several occasions and had seen Mimi each time, usually through the order window, as she did most of the cooking and left waiting tables to others.

She couldn't be any older than Gerard and was pretty, even when wearing one of those weird chef's hats and a hairnet. He'd heard she'd been a high-powered chef in New Orleans at one point and had given it all up to move to Bayou Mambaloa and take over her aunt's diner, her aunt being the original Tante Mimi.

Rumor had it that the second iteration of Mimi's had suffered a big breakup with a restaurant owner and had tucked her tail and run.

As far as Gerard was concerned, it was New Orleans' loss and Bayou Mambaloa's gain. Everything Mimi prepared was amazing, even simple scrambled eggs and toast.

The diner door opened. Deputy Taylor and Sheriff Bergeron entered and came straight to their table.

Mimi showed up a moment later, carrying a tray with a pot of coffee and four mugs. She set the mugs in front of each of her guests, poured the coffee and left them to talk.

Sheriff Bergeron leaned forward. "Deputy Taylor said you needed to talk to me. Something about your dog?"

Bernie opened her mouth, but her eyes filled with tears, and she turned to Gerard. "Tell him,"

Gerard filled the sheriff in on all that had transpired through the night and what they'd found that morning. He left out the part about making love to his client. That was strictly on a need-to-know basis. Nobody but him and Bernie needed to know about that.

"I'll get out there after this meeting and look around," Deputy Taylor said.

"Have you had any more contact with the resort broker?" the sheriff asked.

Bernie shook her head. "Not over the last week. I've had a few real estate agents leave messages, wanting to know if I was willing to sell the property. I don't respond."

"Can you send me the numbers for them?" Sheriff Bergeron asked.

"Sorry," Bernie grimaced. "I deleted them."

Gerard pushed back from the table. "I'll be right back. I need to report to my boss. He'll want to know what's going on." He touched Bernie's arm. "Will you be okay?"

She nodded.

He stepped out the front door of the diner and called Remy.

Remy answered on the first ring. "Gerard, give me a situation report. Shelby said there was another attack at the farm. Something about a dog?"

Gerard told him what had happened. "Whoever is doing this is getting more brazen," he said.

"We need surveillance," Remy said.

"I was thinking cameras placed strategically would help us identify the culprit," Gerard suggested. "Maybe a game camera on the pigpen since there wouldn't be any electricity to tap into. The sooner, the better."

"I'll see what I can do to have cameras installed today."

"Thanks," Gerard said. "Also, it would be great if the guys could get out there ASAP to help with the cleanup and see if there's anything to salvage after the sheriff's department checks it out."

"I can make that happen," Remy assured him. "They were due out there at noon anyway. We'll move up the timeline."

"Remy, have you heard anything from Swede about the resort wanting to purchase Bellamy Acres? Or about the company trying to broker the deal?"

"Not much more than we already knew," Remy said. "When I spoke with Swede last night, he was digging into the men working the deal. He hoped to have more information later today."

"What about the foot? I don't see how it relates to the attempts to purchase the property unless they hope to scare Bernie into selling."

"Maybe poisoning her dog is supposed to drive home their death threat," Remy suggested.

"Nothing makes sense," Gerard said. "We need to catch whoever is messing with her. Preferably before they follow through on their threat."

"I hear ya," Remy said. "I'll work on the surveillance cameras and get the guys out there to work on cleanup and harvesting the rest of the melons. I'll be out there as soon as I can to help."

"Thanks." Gerard ended the call and returned to the diner as Mimi laid two full plates on the table.

"Perfect timing," she said with a smile.

The sheriff and Deputy Taylor stood.

"We'll leave you two to your breakfast," the sheriff said.

"I'd like to be there when you come out to see the damage," Bernie said.

"I have a few things I want to check on at the office, and then we'll head out there. That should give you time to finish your meal."

"Thank you," Bernie said. "I hate to be a bother."

"You're not the bother," Deputy Taylor said. "You aren't the one causing problems."

"Yeah, but if I'd just agreed to sell the place, none of this would be happening." Bernie gave a weak smile. "They wouldn't have felt the need to kill Gertrude and poison Howey."

"You can't blame yourself for the actions of others," the sheriff said. "We'll get to the bottom of this and bring the criminals to justice."

On that note, the sheriff and deputy left the diner.

Bernie's gaze followed them. "I hope they're right."

"One way or another, we will resolve this issue," he promised.

"Please, make it sooner than later," she said. "I'm beginning to think I need to move my animals to a safer location until then."

Gerard couldn't argue with her suggestion. Until they got a handle on who was doing the damage, they couldn't stop it from happening. They needed that surveillance equipment ASAP. Either that, or he'd go on stakeout all night long to nab the bastard—if he showed up. Based on the pig releases, they knew he'd been there two nights in a row. He could show up again.

Gerard cleaned his plate of the delicious breakfast Mimi had provided, the best omelet he'd eaten his entire life.

Bernie, on the other hand, picked at the food on

her plate. She nibbled a few bites and drank her entire cup of coffee.

Gerard worried the stress was getting to her. The attack on Howey had gutted her. With the loss of a significant portion of her crop, she now had to worry about how she'd pay her taxes and purchase food for her animals.

He had some money in his savings. Not much since he'd used a big portion of it to pay off his mother's house in Mississippi. She'd gone to college after her divorce was final, earning her counseling degree.

Without worrying about a mortgage, she could pay her own bills and save for her retirement. She'd joined the singles group at her local church and had made several friends. She seemed happy for the first time in her life, which made Gerard happy for her.

Whatever money he had in his savings, he could give to Bernie to help her make ends meet until she could recoup her losses.

But when would that be? A year from now?

Being a farmer was hard enough without someone destroying her crop.

Gerard insisted on driving the old truck back to the farm with a quick stop at the boarding house so that he could grab more clothes, his night vision goggles and more ammunition for his pistol.

He was surprised Bernie didn't put up a fight

about him driving. She sat quietly in the passenger seat, a permanent crease across her forehead.

He wanted to tell her everything would be all right, but he couldn't tell her when that might be. The frustration of being unable to put a name to the threats she'd gotten was getting to him.

At the boarding house, he parked close to the door. As old as the truck was, it didn't have air conditioning. The day was warming quickly, making the interior hot and humid.

"Do you want to come up and wait in my room while I grab my stuff?" he asked. "It'll be a lot cooler than sitting out here."

She shook her head, rolling the window all the way down. "I'll be okay."

Gerard shut off the engine and rolled down his window as well. "I won't be long." He dropped down from the truck and strode into the building and up the stairs to his room. He grabbed a gym bag and shoved clothes from the closet and the dresser into the bag, along with the night vision goggles, the bullet-proof vest and the radio headset. Better to have it and not need it than not have it and need it. He shoved a pair of combat boots in and a packet of condoms.

Last night, he'd told himself the previous night would be a one-time affair. He'd blown that vow this morning when he'd made love with Bernie all over again. He knew it was just going to make it harder when he did make the break, but...

Better to have protection and not need it than not have it and need it.

Less than five minutes later, he descended the stairs and jogged out to the truck.

Bernie wasn't where he'd left her in the passenger seat.

His heart skipped several beats before he saw movement out of the corner of his eye.

Bernie stood in the shade of a sycamore tree, her cell phone pressed to her ear. "That's good to know," she said, a small smile curling her lips. "Thank you, Dr. Saulnier." She ended the call and turned to Gerard, a full-on smile spreading across her face.

She absolutely glowed, her joy so beautiful it hit him full in the gut.

He pressed a hand to his belly. "Was that the vet?"

She walked toward him. "Howey's awake and eating."

When he opened his arms, she walked into them. She pressed her cheek to his chest and wrapped her arms around his waist.

Bernie fit against him so perfectly that holding her felt like...home. That thought sucked all the air from his lungs. It took a full minute of holding her before he could find and use his voice again. "That's good to know. Do we need to stop by the vet's office and pick him up?"

She shook her head without moving it from his chest. "No. The vet wants to continue monitoring him through the night and ensure whatever was in his system is flushed out before I take him home." She sighed. "And he's probably better off at the vet's office. At least he won't be poisoned there."

Gerard's arms tightened around her. "Ready to go home?"

She nodded but didn't make a move to leave his embrace. Then she shook her head. "No. I'm not ready."

"We don't have to go there. We could stay in town and go to Broussard's, buy candy bars and sodas, then head down to the marina and sit on the dock with our feet in the water."

She leaned back and smiled into his eyes. "That sounds good, all the way up to dangling our feet in the water."

"What? You don't like getting your feet wet in anything but mud?"

She laughed. "No. I love getting my feet wet. It's just that there are a couple of alligators that like to hang out by the marina looking for some of the chum the fisherman throw into the water after cleaning their catches of the day. I wouldn't want them to mistake my bare feet for chum and take a bite. But if you feel the need to dangle your toes in alligator-infested waters, by all means, knock yourself out."

"Smart ass," he grumbled. "Way to shoot down a perfectly good date idea with a little reality." He pressed a kiss to her forehead. "Since you're not with me on the dock dangling, can I interest you in heading out to beautiful Bellamy Acres for the joy of picking a thousand watermelons?"

"You really know how to sweep a girl off her feet, don't you?"

He bent and swung her up into his arms. "I might not know much about animals and farm life, but I can sweep you up in my arms."

She giggled. "I give you an A for effort and style. Now, you can put me down before you strain something. I'm not a petite little thing like most women."

"No, you're not," he said. "And that's a good thing. I usually look like a dirty old man with a little girl when I date petite women. You're the perfect height and weight. I don't feel like I'll break you if I bump against you accidentally."

Her brow twisted. "Thank you, I think."

"Yes, that was my awkward attempt at a compliment." He carried her to the truck.

She pulled the handle to open the door, and he deposited her on the passenger seat.

This time, when he leaned in to buckle her belt, she caught his cheeks between her palms and kissed him. "Thank you."

"For buckling your seatbelt?" He nodded. "You're welcome."

"Thank you for being here," she said. "I know I'm your assignment and all, but it's nice to have someone to lean on, even if it's only for a short time."

"It's my pleasure." He kissed her full on the lips, then backed out, closed the door and rounded to the driver's side. A knot had formed in his gut at her words.

Bernie had been on her own since her husband's death, managing a farm, animals and bills with no one else to help. He admired her for her strength and determination and realized how hard it must have been to power through while also bearing the burden of grief.

For a brief, foolish moment, he wished he could be there for her always. To help her with the work, share the expenses and come up with solutions when things didn't go right.

She needed someone by her side.

But that someone wasn't him.

It couldn't be. His genes were tainted. Instead of relieving her burden, he could be adding to it. She'd be better off without him and open to falling in love with a better man.

The thought of her with someone else stuck like a knife in his chest. Even though she didn't belong to him. Couldn't belong to him.

Silence reigned in the cab of the old truck, the only sound the roar of the wind blowing through the open windows.

When Gerard drove around the side of the house into the barnyard, Bernie gasped.

"What are all of these people doing here?"

The barnyard was full of vehicles and people.

"I asked Remy to send the team out earlier than noon to help clean up and start picking the rest of the melons. That accounts for half of the people. And there's the sheriff and Deputy Taylor. I don't know the rest of these folks."

Bernie frowned. "I do. They're friends and neighbors. But what are they doing here?" She slipped out of the passenger seat onto the ground.

Gerard climbed down from the truck and joined her as she approached the small crowd.

Tante Mimi and Deputy Taylor approached Bernie with two other women.

Deputy Taylor gave Bernie a lopsided grin. "You know, when word gets around that one of our own is having trouble, you can't keep good people away."

Bernie shook her head. "I don't understand."

"Gisele, Felina and Mimi asked how they could help." Deputy Taylor raised her hands. "I said you might need help cleaning up the mess and harvesting the rest of the melons. Mimi reminded me that tomorrow is the weekend Farmer's Market in town. I bet you haven't had time to think about that."

"I haven't," Bernie admitted. "I figured I wouldn't make it with everything going on here."

"You have to make it," the woman Gerard recognized as the gift shop owner, Gisele, stepped forward. "The community relies on you to provide first-class produce for their homes."

"There will be plenty of other farmers there to do the same," Bernie insisted.

"But none of them will be from Bellamy Acres," the woman beside Gisele said. She smiled at Gerard and held out her hand. "I'm Felina Faivre. And you're the yummy bodyguard I've heard about."

"Gerard Guidry." He shook her hand, his brow furrowing. "I don't know about yummy, but it's nice to meet you."

"Believe me," Felina said. "The pleasure's mine."

"I appreciate the sentiment," Bernie said, "but I can't ask all of you to sacrifice your business hours to bail me out. I mean, geez, Gisele, who's minding the gift shop while you're out here?"

"I hung the Out-to-Lunch sign on my door." Gisele lifted her face to the sun. "It's too nice a day to be stuck inside."

Bernie turned to Felina. "What about your flower shop? Tell me you didn't close it on my account?"

Felina shrugged. "It was a slow day. I'm not missing anything. People can leave orders on my voice mail or go online."

"The point is, we came to help," Mimi said. "Shut up and let us do that. We even brought more people to get it done quickly."

Gerard's chest swelled at the community's outpouring of support for Bernie and Bellamy Acres.

Deputy Taylor nodded toward the trailer with the boxes of destroyed melons. "We made a thorough check around the barnyard, in the barn where you found Howey and out near the pigpen and didn't find anything that would point to who did this. We dusted the door handle on the barn and will take the prints back to the station and hope to find a match. Other than that, there's not much else we can do."

Remy appeared. "Are we clear to start the cleanup?"

Deputy Taylor cocked an eyebrow. "It's up to Bernie."

Bernie's lips twisted. "Might as well." She dug in her purse for the keys to the truck and handed them to Remy. "Take the trailer out to the pigpen and shovel as much as you can of what's in the boxes over the fence. Penelope and the gang will finally get what they've been trying to get to these past two nights."

Remy nodded. "Got it." He tipped his head toward Gerard. "I couldn't get anyone to install the surveillance system today, but I've got someone coming out first thing in the morning."

Gerard nodded. "Bernie and I will be at the farmer's market in the morning and unable to meet with the guy. I believe the market closes around two."

"I'll see if he can adjust his schedule so you and Bernie will be there. In the meantime, we have work to do here." Remy returned to the trailer of ruined watermelons.

He sent a couple of guys into the barn. They returned with shovels and pitchforks and loaded them onto the trailer. While most of Gerard's team climbed onto the back of the trailer, Lucas slipped into the passenger seat. Remy slid behind the wheel and drove the truck across the field to the pigpen.

"You didn't want to go with them?" Bernie asked.

Gerard shook his head. "Sweetheart, I'm your shadow. Where you go, I go."

"Tell us what you need done, and we'll get to work on it," Mimi said.

Bernie split the volunteers into two groups, sending half out to the watermelon patch to start picking and lining up the melons for when Gerard's team had the trailer cleared of the smashed fruit and loaded with clean, dry boxes.

The other half of the volunteers were given bushel baskets and directed into a separate garden where Bernie had grown a wide variety of produce. She parked the modified produce truck close to the garden and instructed the volunteers to fill the labeled bins with the appropriate vegetables.

She pointed Gerard in the direction of several long rows of cornstalks and showed him how to tell what was ripe and how to strip the ears of corn off the stalk. Bernie worked another row parallel to his. Before long, they'd picked all the ripe corn and loaded it into the bin labeled CORN. When the bin was completely full, they loaded the remaining bushels into the back of the truck, sliding them beneath the bins on the side.

While they were picking corn, Remy and his guys finished dumping the broken melons and rinds into the pigpen, stacked the ruined boxes on the edge of the field to be burned later and returned to the barn to load fresh, empty boxes onto the trailer.

With more hands helping, they finished harvesting the ripe watermelons in record time, completing the task just after noon.

Once the produce truck was full, Bernie parked it in the barn, where it would stay cooler than in the sun until the morning when she would take it to the farmer's market.

Gerard marveled at how willing the people of Bayou Mambaloa were to contribute their time and effort to help a friend and neighbor.

Bernie hugged each volunteer and thanked them. When she tried to send them home with vegetables, they declined. "Save them for the market tomorrow," they said.

Gerard stood back while Bernie made her rounds, keeping a close eye on her. Not that he thought any of these people were the ones causing trouble. But he couldn't be too careful.

"She's special," a voice said beside him.

He turned to find the dark-haired, dark-skinned Gisele beside him.

"Yes, she is," he agreed.

"All her life, she's given so much of herself, caring for others, it's about time someone took care of her." Gisele looked up at him with her strangely golden eyes. "You'll be good for her and give her the babies she always wanted."

Gerard frowned. When he opened his mouth to disavow her of her prediction, she raised a finger, cutting him off before he could start.

"She has seen enough grief for one lifetime." Gisele's eyes narrowed into slits. "If you break her heart, I will put a spell on you that will make your balls shrivel and your dick shrink to the size of a worm." She held his gaze with hers a moment longer. Then her eyes widened, and a sweet smile transformed her face. "I'm glad we had this conversation."

Bernie approached, glancing from Gisele to Gerard and back. "Everything all right?"

Gisele patted Gerard's cheek. "Perfectly. We were just getting to know each other."

CHAPTER 9

BERNIE'S GAZE went from Gisele to Gerard.

The man was frowning at something Gisele had said.

Bernie leaned close to Gisele. "What did you say to him?"

Gisele hugged Bernie. "Just that we love you, sweetie."

Bernie bet that wasn't all she'd said.

Mimi, Felina and Shelby joined them at that moment.

"We all love you," Shelby said. "I just feel like we haven't done enough."

Bernie laughed as her eyes filled with tears. "You've done more than enough."

Mimi shook her head. "Maybe. But I'm sure there's more that can be done."

"No. Really." Bernie looked around at the women who'd joined forces for her. "I've been a terrible friend these past few years, and you still came out to help. I don't know what I did to deserve you."

"You've always been there when someone needed extra food on their table, offering fresh produce and meat from your freezer," Mimi said.

"And you're kind to animals," Felina said, "taking in strays, big and small, finding loving homes for them either here on the farm or with other people who care."

Bernie's cheeks heated, and her heart swelled at the outpouring of love. "I don't do any more than anyone else. And lately, I've been so busy I barely have time to wave hello. I'm sorry for being so preoccupied. You all mean so much to me. You're my family, and I love you all."

The women closed in for a group hug, laughing and promising to get together soon for drinks at the Crawdad Hole.

When they broke apart, Shelby waved Bernie and Gerard toward the truck with the loaded trailer. "Get going. If you leave now, you should be back before dark."

Bernie thanked them one more time and climbed into the driver's seat.

Gerard stepped up to her window. "Are you sure you don't want me to drive?"

"I'm sure," she said. "I'm used to driving this route with a trailer. You'd do fine, but I'd feel better in the driver's seat. I have a lot riding on this load."

Gerard walked around the front of the truck and climbed into the passenger seat.

As Bernie drove out of the barnyard, Gerard looked back at the people standing around.

Bernie glanced in the side mirror, expecting the crowd to disperse and head home. But they hadn't. In fact, they were huddled together as if they were going to visit for a while before heading back to town.

Bernie smiled and wished she could have stayed and spent time with them. She needed to make time to be with her friends and neighbors. She'd forgotten how much she enjoyed visiting with them.

Bernie drove out the gate onto the highway, her heart full and almost right with the world after all that had happened. "I can't get over everyone showing up to help."

"They care about you," Gerard said.

She smiled. "Yes. They do." Her brow puckered as she recalled his conversation with her friend. "What was Gisele saying to you when I walked up?"

"Nothing important," he said without meeting her gaze.

"Must've been important enough," Bernie said. "You were frowning."

His lips twisted. "Let's just say she was showing her love for you."

"Gisele is the granddaughter of Bayou Mambaloa's Voodoo queen." Bernie shot a suspicious look his way. "She didn't threaten to put a spell on you, did she?"

Gerard clamped his lips shut and stared at the road ahead.

"She did." Bernie laughed. "Did she threaten to turn you into a frog? Or to make you cross-eyed forever?"

"No," he said. He shot a worried frown in her direction. "Has she done that to anyone else?"

"When we were in high school, a boy cheated on one of Gisele's friends. After she found out about it, that boy mysteriously croaked like a frog for an entire week before he got his voice back." Bernie shrugged. "Some say it was a coincidence."

Gerard frowned. "What do you think?"

She gave him a pointed look. "I keep an open mind. And I'm careful not to piss off the Voodoo queen or her granddaughter."

Gerard's face blanched, and he laid his hand over his crotch.

Bernie glanced at him again. "She really got to you, didn't she?" She touched his arm. "Don't worry. She can't hurt you. She likes to put the fear of

Voodoo in everyone. It's a wall she builds around herself to keep from being hurt."

"Gisele's afraid of being hurt?" Gerard blinked. "I'm sure most people are afraid she'll hurt them."

"Her evil Voodoo persona is just an act. She's really sweet and has a big heart," Bernie said. "Unfortunately, someone broke it a while back. She hasn't let anyone else close enough to risk it again. It happened shortly after Ray died. She needed a place to get away for a few days. I needed someone to think about besides myself. She stayed with me for a week. We wallowed in sadness, drank wine and were there for each other."

"Well, she's still there for you," Gerard said, his tone flat.

"Ah. She warned you not to hurt me." Bernie nodded. "Don't worry. You were upfront with me about your views on relationships. I went into this with my eyes wide open. Rest assured. I'll be fine when you leave. No broken heart. No throwing myself at your feet, begging you to stay. I'll consider you practice for when I really do get back out there and open myself up to dating." She gave him a brief smile. "So, you see, you're doing me a favor by giving me a taste of what I've been missing and showing me it really is like riding a bicycle. You never forget how to do it. You just get back on and ride. Right?"

"Right," Gerard grunted. "Easy as riding a freaking bicycle."

"That's right." Bernie nodded smugly. She'd been approaching Gerard wrong all along. The man had convinced himself he wasn't the right man for her. She'd already proved they were highly compatible in bed. She'd so convinced him that they were good in the sex department that he'd gone for morning sex with little encouragement.

She smiled to herself. A little reverse psychology might just do the trick. All the talk about her time spent with him being nothing more than a practice round would either get to him or prove he really wasn't committed and never would be.

Based on how he was scowling, Bernie guessed he wasn't thrilled with her talking about dating other men and having sex with them after *practicing* with Gerard.

Apparently, he was used to walking away and not looking back.

She had to make sure that when he walked away this time, he not only looked back but came back.

The drive to New Orleans went quickly. Since it was the middle of the day, the traffic was lighter than in the morning when everyone was hurrying to get into the city to work or in the afternoon when everyone was heading home.

They would arrive at the distribution center in time to unload the boxes and get back on the road home before rush hour.

Bernie's distributor wasn't happy that she'd only brought half the watermelons promised. And the price he paid was less than she'd expected. Definitely not enough to cover the taxes and put money aside to pay her personal income taxes in April.

Her only hope now was to sell a lot of produce at the farmer's market over the next couple of weeks and to Broussard's Country Store and the small grocery stores in the neighboring towns. She didn't sell a lot at any one location, which, in turn, meant she didn't make a lot of money. But everything would add up if she was very frugal with her spending, canned food to see her through to the next harvest and sold some of the pigs. She might make it. *If* the trucks and tractor didn't break down *and* the well pump limped along for another year *and* the weather cooperated. She'd already canceled her cable, telephone landline and dropped down to the minimum she could manage on internet and cell phone service. She could cut back on the air conditioning to save on her electric bill and burn wood in her fireplace instead of gas heat during the winter.

When they arrived at the farm, Bernie backed the empty trailer into the row of implements.

After Gerard jumped down to disengage the hitch and lights, Bernie pulled forward a few inches and parked the truck. She slid out of the truck and slung her purse over her shoulder.

Gerard met her in front of the truck and held out his arm.

She slipped her hand through the crook of his elbow and smiled up at him. "I'll feed the animals and then whip something up for dinner."

"*We'll* feed the animals," Gerard said. "Then, either *I'll* make dinner, or *we'll* cook dinner together."

Bernie leaned into him. "Mmm. I like that thought of us cooking together...naked. Do you know I've never had sex on a countertop? And this morning was the first time I've done it doggy-style."

Gerard glanced over at her, the corners of his mouth twitching. "Are you serious?"

She nodded. "Serious as sin. I know you plan on bugging out when this assignment is over, but while you're here, could we practice some of the positions I'm sorely lacking any experience with?"

Gerard groaned. "Keep talking like that, and I'll introduce you to sex against the wall."

She stepped in front of him, pressing her breasts against his chest. "Promise?" she said in her lowest, sexist tone.

"Woman," he said, his jaw tight. "Not out here. We

don't know if the guy who's been behind the attacks is watching us as we speak. I refuse to give him the satisfaction of a free porn show."

"You do have a good point." Bernie slid her hand into his back pocket and squeezed his ass. "But the cooking naked? We're a go for that?" She smiled up at him as innocently as she could while talking about cooking in the nude.

"You're on," he said.

"Then hurry," she said and picked up the pace. "We can't start supper until the animals are fed. I also want to check the pigpen to make sure they can't get out of their enclosure. Not that there are many more melons to protect. But I would like to have some for the farmers market over the next few weeks.

"I'll get feed for the chickens while you collect the eggs," she said and hurried toward the barn. "Don't forget the fishnet."

"Fishnet?" Gerard's brow dipped and then came back up. "Oh yeah. The rooster."

Bernie hurried into the barn, scooped a bucket of chicken feed and carried it out of the barn and into the chicken coop, passing the rooster where Gerard had hung it in the fishnet on a hook.

She chuckled as she recalled the look of confusion on his face when she'd first mentioned the fishnet.

"You've never been around a farm before now, have you?"

"Never," he admitted as he plucked eggs from the nests and carefully laid them in the bucket Bernie used for that purpose.

"What about pets?" she asked.

His lips pressed into a line. "My dad wouldn't let me have a pet."

"Not even a dog?"

"I learned quickly how serious he was about no animals in the house or yard. I found a stray puppy in the field close to our house and brought it home. I begged my father to let me keep it. He took that puppy from me and drowned it." He shook his head. "I'll never forget what he did. And I never forgave him."

"That's horrible." Bernie touched his arm. "I'm so sorry."

"He drank so much that night he almost beat my mother to death. When I tried to stop him, he flung me against the wall and kicked me until he broke one of my ribs. I guess he figured he could beat the thought of that puppy out of my head. It worked. I never brought a puppy back to his house."

Bernie poured the chicken feed into the feeder. "Makes you wonder what happened to your father to make him the way he was."

"I stopped caring anything about him at a very young age. In fact, I went the complete opposite direction and wished he would die." He collected the last egg and followed her out of the chicken coop.

They fed Lucy and Desi, the llamas, Dom DeLuise the donkey and the goats. When it came time to check the pigpen, Bernie opted to take the four-wheeler.

It seemed to suit Gerard just fine. He rode on the back with his arms wrapped tightly around Bernie's waist the entire way.

The pigpen was the same as it had been the night before when they'd herded the escapees back inside their home.

Bernie checked the latch on the gate. It was secure but not enough. She returned to the four-wheeler, unlocked a cable from the back rack, wrapped it around the gate and the brace post and pressed the lock together tightly.

Her lips twisted wryly. "A bolt cutter would cut right through that, but maybe it will slow them down."

By the time they returned to the house, dusk had settled over the land.

Bernie's pulse kicked into high gear. Cooking naked was next on her list.

"Last one in the house has to wear an apron," Bernie called out, and she leaped forward.

Not to be left too far behind, Gerard raced to catch up to her before they reached the porch steps.

Gerard caught her around the middle and swung her around and into his arms, kissing her soundly.

"Eh-hmm," a voice sounded from the shadows on the porch. "I was going to announce our presence earlier, but you were a little preoccupied, and I didn't want to interrupt."

Gerard stepped between Bernie and the porch.

Two men moved out of the shadows and descended the porch, their faces becoming clear in the fading light.

Bernie recognized the man on the left dressed in khaki slacks and a white polo shirt. He'd slicked back his thick blond hair, displaying his model-perfect facial features. Bobby Burns had been a senior when Bernie was a Freshman in high school. As the star quarterback on the football team, he'd been the most popular student in the school. And he knew it.

The other man wore a tailored gray suit with a light blue shirt and graphite-gray tie. With salt-and-pepper gray hair and blue eyes, most women would consider him a silver fox.

Bernie considered him a trespasser and wanted him gone. She frowned and moved up to stand beside Gerard. "Bobby, we have nothing to talk about. I'm not selling Bellamy Acres."

"Bernie, at least talk with my client, Mr. Jonathon Worthington of Worthington Brokerage Firm. He wanted to speak with you himself and let you know what Grand Bijou's plans are for this property and those surrounding it."

"I've already spoken to two of his firm's salesmen." Bernie held up her hand. "I'm sorry, Mr. Worthington. Bobby is wasting your time. I'm not selling Bellamy Acres. Nothing you can say will change my mind." She started to walk past him.

Worthington stepped in front of her.

Gerard tensed beside Bernie. "That's one," he murmured beneath his breath.

Bernie shot a glance at her Marine. His jaw was tight, and his fists were clenched.

"Ms. Bellamy," Worthington said, "I understand this was your husband's heritage. Land that has been in his family for over a century. I'm so sorry for your loss."

"Thank you. Now, if you'll excuse me, I'm tired and need a shower." She stepped to the side.

Worthington stepped in front of her again.

Beside Bernie, Gerard murmured. "Two."

Worthington continued, "Grand Bijou Resorts is poised to sink a lot of money into Bayou Mambaloa. Positioning the resort here will create hundreds of jobs at the resort as well as for the businesses throughout the town."

She crossed her arms over her chest. "That's nice. But it won't be on my property."

The man's brow dipped. "We understand that

when the boat factory closed, the town lost its major employer, and people had to leave to find work. Building a Grand Bijou Resort in Bayou Mambaloa will revive the town, the economy and keep young people from leaving."

Bernie sighed. "Look, Mr. Worthington..."

He smiled. "Please, call me Jonathon."

She didn't want to call him anything as she wouldn't be seeing him ever again and didn't want to get to know the guy.

"Look, Mr. Worthington," she said, holding onto her temper by a thread. "I heard this exact sales job from Bobby, verbatim. Now. Read my lips. Bellamy Acres. Is Not. For Sale." Her eyes narrowed, and she stepped closer until she was practically nose-to-nose with the man. She poked her finger into his fancy tie. "And if you, or anyone else, hurts another one of my animals or tries to sabotage my property again in any way, I'll find you, and I'll make you pay."

"I don't know what you're talking about." Worthington raised his hands and gripped Bernie's arms. "I'm not threatening you. You're threatening me."

"Three," Gerard said. He moved around Bernie, grabbed Worthington by his tailored lapels and jerked him away from Bernie. He shot her a quick glance. "I know you can handle this, but he hit my limit."

She fought a smile. "By all means. He's not listening to me."

Gerard glared at the broker. "You should listen to the woman. She's not selling her place. No amount of sabotage or death threats is going to change her mind. As her bodyguard, if I find you on her property again, I'll perceive it as a threat, and I'll do whatever it takes to neutralize that threat, including but not limited to shooting, breaking bones, and feeding the perpetrator to the alligators." He lifted the man by his suit. "Do I make myself clear?"

Worthington's eyes were wide, and his face had paled. "Yes...yes, you do."

Gerard held him there a moment longer and then shoved him away.

Worthington staggered backward several steps. Once he had his balance, he straightened his tie and suit jacket. He looked past Gerard to Bernie. "If you change your mind—"

Gerard stepped toward him, emitting a menacing growl.

Bobbie and Worthington scurried toward a black SUV with a Burns Realty sign affixed to the door. When they were safely inside, Bobbie spun the vehicle around and kicked up gravel as they left Bellamy Acres.

Bernie laughed. "Did you really growl at the broker?"

Gerard's lips twitched. "I wanted to hit him, but he would've had to swing first. The growl wasn't as satisfying as plowing my fist into his face, but it did release some of my anger."

Bernie slipped her hand through his arm. "See? You don't give yourself enough credit. You wanted to punch that guy, but you didn't. You're a good man, Gerard Guidry."

Gerard frowned. "Just because I didn't hit the guy doesn't mean I wouldn't lose control in a different situation."

She leaned into him. "I think you are in complete control and would only use force if it was absolutely necessary." She sighed. "Damn them for showing up when they did."

Gerard walked with her up the steps. "Killed the mood, didn't it?"

She nodded. "Right now, I'd settle for a peanut butter and jelly sandwich, a shower and bed."

"You're in luck," he said. "PBJ is one of my specialties." Once in the house, he turned her to face him. "Go get your shower. I'll whip up the sandwiches, and we can make it an early night."

She nodded. "I have to be up before dawn to get to the farmer's market and set up. People are early risers on market days. They like to beat the heat."

He pressed a kiss to her forehead. "You're beautiful when you're fierce."

Her heart warmed. "Should I be fierce more often?"

Gerard stared down into her eyes. "You're beautiful even when you're not fierce." He tipped her chin up and lightly brushed his lips across hers.

Bernie wrapped her arms around his neck and pulled him closer, deepening the kiss, her body melting against his. When they finally broke apart, she smiled up at him. "I want a raincheck on cooking naked."

He chuckled. "You got it."

With her heart light, she practically floated to the bathroom.

Gerard thought she was beautiful.

As she washed her hair and body, her thoughts went back to her encounter with Bobbie Burns and Jonathon Worthington. She suspected the broker liked to win.

Was he ruthless enough to hire people to make her life so miserable she'd be forced to sell?

Hopefully, he'd gotten the message and would move on.

Bernie was tired. The stress of her financial situation was secondary to the worry about the animals in her care.

If Worthington wasn't going to back down on his efforts to purchase her property, would he or his lackey be back to try something else to get her to sell?

As she stepped out of the shower, she made up her mind. She needed sleep, but her farm needed her awake more.

After she and Gerard retired for the night, she'd slip out with her shotgun and spend the night on the back porch, where she could watch the barn and the fields for intruders.

CHAPTER 10

GERARD HADN'T PURSUED sex with Bernie after they'd finished their sandwiches and brushed their teeth. He'd tried to sleep on the couch, but Bernie wouldn't hear of it, insisting he sleep with her.

Granted, she didn't have to twist his arm.

He liked how she felt pressed against his side and had to concentrate to keep from getting a boner.

She needed sleep. The stress of the continued attacks and then the altercation with the broker had to be taking its toll on her.

He pulled her close and held her until her breathing became more even and her body relaxed.

Once he was certain she was asleep, Gerard eased out of the bed, gathered his clothes and gun and moved into the living room to dress. He'd retrieved his night vision goggles from the gym bag, looped the strap over his neck and tiptoed to the door, carrying his boots.

He'd just reached for the front doorknob when a floorboard creaked behind him.

Gerard spun.

Bernie entered the living room from her bedroom dressed in the worn T-shirt, the shorts she'd worn to bed and her dingo boots. In her hands was her shotgun.

"You should stay in the house," he whispered.

"Yeah," she said. "That's not going to happen. Over the past two nights, they've turned my pigs loose, destroyed my property and poisoned my dog. I really hope they're back tonight because I'll be waiting."

"That was my plan. No need for both of us to lose sleep."

She snorted and closed the distance between them. "I won't sleep, knowing they might be back. I want a shot at catching them in the act."

"Same," Gerard said. "We need to put an end to this."

"So, I'm not going back to bed," she said. "How do you want to play this?"

"We could both hang out on the porch and watch for movement," Gerard said.

"Pretend I'm one of your Marine teammates. What would you do?"

"I'd have him positioned where he could see the

house and barn. Then, I'd go out to the field and lay low in the shadows where I could monitor the back of the barn and the pigpen. Plus, we'd keep in touch via radio headsets. I only have one radio headset."

"You have a cell phone. I have a cell phone. If something goes south near one, we could call the other," she offered.

Gerard's lips pressed together. "I don't feel right leaving you alone unless you're locked safely in the house."

"And I'm not going to stay in the house and do nothing while someone attacks my animals and property." She lifted her chin. "I'm a good shot."

"I'm sure you are." Gerard didn't like her being exposed to the attacker, but he didn't have a choice. "We can both hang out close to the house and see what happens."

She shook her head. "Someone needs to stay close to the house and barn, and someone else should be where they can see what's happening with the pigs. If you want to stay by the house, I'll guard the pigs." She reached for the doorknob.

His hand closed over hers. "You're a stubborn woman," he said.

She lifted her chin. "I've had to be to survive."

He bent and captured her mouth with his in a quick, hard kiss. "Don't change a thing. But for tonight, you've got the house; I'll take the field. Deal?"

She nodded. "Deal."

They slipped out the door. Clinging to the shadows, they moved around to the corner of the house.

Gerard pointed to a large bush.

Bernie slipped into the shadows and hunkered low. From her position, she would be able to see two sides of the house, the front of the barn and the pasture where the llamas, donkey and goats lived.

Gerard slipped through the shadows and along the edge of the watermelon field to a point where he could watch the pigpen and the back of the barn. He could just see the corner of the house where Bernie lay hidden in the bushes.

Now, all they had to do was wait.

An hour passed.

His phone, on silent, vibrated in his front pocket. He leaned over his phone, covering it so that no light would shine out from his position, and read the message.

Anything?

He grinned.

Bernie was someone who liked to get things done. Sitting still for hours on a stakeout had to be driving her nuts.

As he replied, he hoped she was shading the light from her phone.

No.

Another hour passed. Thankfully, a light breeze

blew across the field, keeping the humidity at a tolerable level.

He'd been looking at the pigpen when something moved in his peripheral vision.

Turning left toward the barn, he lifted his night vision goggles and spotted the green silhouette of a man near the rear of the barn. He was hunched over, carrying something, shaking it as he worked his way around to the front corner.

A branch snapped in the opposite direction from the barn.

Gerard started to turn his goggles in that direction but stopped when a flame ignited in the hands of the figure by the barn.

He'd lit a match.

As quickly as the flame ignited, the breeze extinguished it. Holy shit. The thing he'd been shaking had been a gas can.

"Fuck!" Gerard dropped the goggles and lunged to his feet.

Footsteps sounded to Gerard's right as if something, or someone, was moving quickly through the woods. He spun, holding his gun out in front of him. He couldn't see into the shadows. Whoever was out there was beating a hasty retreat.

He didn't have time to worry about whoever was moving away. Not when the barn was about to go up in flames. He ran toward the barn but wouldn't make it there in time to stop the man from setting it aflame.

The arsonist lit another match. Before he could throw it on the gasoline, a shot rang out.

The man staggered backward.

Still running, Gerard held his breath as the match fell from the man's fingers. The flame disappeared before it hit the ground.

Gerard didn't slow, running straight for the corner of the house where he'd left Bernie, kicking himself for leaving her alone. What the hell kind of protector was he if he wasn't protecting his charge?

He was several yards from her position, frantically scanning the shadows for any sign of her. "Bernie," he called out as he slowed to a stop.

Her head popped out of the shadows. "Gerard, did you get him?"

He stared down at her. "Get him?"

"You fired a shot," she said.

"No. I didn't," he said and dove into the bush beside her. "It wasn't you?"

She shook her head. "No. I saw movement to the right of the barn, but I didn't have a clear shot and wasn't going to shoot in case it was Dom or one of the dark goats. If you didn't shoot, who did?"

"I don't know, but whoever did nailed a guy on the far side of the barn before he could burn it down."

"What?" Bernie started to rise.

"I need you to stay here and dial 911. Get the sheriff and an ambulance," he said. "I'm going to check it out."

She grabbed his arm before he could leave the shadows. "Be careful. You still owe me a raincheck for naked cooking."

"I wouldn't miss that for anything." He left the bush and darted across the barnyard and into the shadow of the barn.

Working his way around to the corner, he peeked around the edge.

A man lay on the ground moaning. "Help me."

Though the guy had almost burned down the barn, Gerard couldn't let him die. He was the first clue they had as to who was behind the attacks.

He didn't know if the gunman was still out there, but he had to get to the man and move him to a more protected position.

He flipped the safety on his pistol and tucked it into his waistband. Then, crouching low, he ran around the side of the barn and dropped down beside the wounded arsonist.

"Help me," he said, reaching out his hand. "I've been shot."

"Where?"

"My leg," he said. "Get me out of here before he shoots again."

"Hold onto my hand; I'm going to drag you around and into the barn, where you'll be safe until help arrives."

Gerard gripped the man's wrist and, staying low, dragged him around the side of the barn.

Before he reached the door, it was flung open.

Bernie stood just inside, moving back to allow him to get the man through the door.

"Sheriff's on the way," she said.

When he cleared the threshold, she shut the door and turned on the lights. She twisted the lock and turned to the man on the ground.

Her eyes widened. "Billie Joe Weems, what the ever-loving hell?"

Billie Joe closed his eyes. "I needed the money," he said. "God, my leg hurts."

Bernie and Gerard bent to examine the wound.

It was bleeding but not profusely.

"Seems to have missed the arteries," Gerard said. "You'll probably live."

Billie Joe moaned. "It hurts."

"You're lucky that match blew out," Gerard said, "or you'd have been lying in the middle of all that gasoline when it burst into flame."

"I'll get some towels." Bernie spun away.

Gerard reached out and grabbed her arm. "Not if it means crossing the barnyard again."

She shook her head. "I keep clean rags out here in

case I need them." Bernie disappeared into the little office in the corner of the barn and reappeared moments later with several old towels.

Gerard pressed a towel to the wound on the man's leg, applying enough pressure to slow the bleeding. "So," he said, "spill it. Who put you up to burning down Ms. Bellamy's barn?"

"It wasn't my idea to burn down the barn," he said, writhing in pain.

"Whose idea was it?" Bernie asked. "You're already in trouble. You might as well take down whoever put you up to it."

"It wasn't supposed to be this way," the young man whined.

"What way was it supposed to be," Gerard demanded, pushing a little harder.

Billie Joe grimaced. "I was just supposed to let the pigs out to eat the watermelons. That's all. I wasn't supposed to burn no barn or get shot."

"Start from the beginning," Bernie said.

"He paid me to open the gate of the pigpen. The pigs were supposed to get out and eat the water-melons so Ms. Bellamy couldn't sell them."

"Only Penelope was loose, and the gate was closed," Bernie said.

"I left it open. They didn't all come running out. I left after the one ran out, figuring the rest would follow." He grimaced, sweat popping out on his face.

"At what point did you kill my goose?" Bernie demanded.

Billie Joe shook his head. "What goose? I don't know what you're talking about."

"The big white bird you killed and left on my porch." Bernie glared at the young man.

"I didn't kill a goose. I didn't sign up to kill anything."

Bernie paced back and forth. "I don't believe you."

"I didn't kill no goose," Billie Joe insisted.

"What happened next?" Gerard pressed.

"Since the pigs didn't eat the watermelons the first night, I opened the pen the second night and shooed them out. Then I had to smash the watermelons that had already been picked. He didn't want you to sell the melons."

Bernie stopped pacing. "And you had to poison my dog to smash the melons?"

He stared up at Bernie, his brow creased. "I didn't see a dog. The trailer was there with the melons. I climbed into each box and jumped up and down until they were all smashed. No dog came out. I thought for sure someone would hear me."

"And since the watermelons made it to the market, you decided to burn down my barn?" Bernie shook her head.

"No," Billie Joe said. "He said that if I didn't do it, he'd turn me over to the sheriff, and I'd go back to jail. I had to do it. My parole officer is going to throw the book at me." He lay back. "I wouldn't have done it, but I needed the money to bail my dog out of the animal shelter. They were going to put him down. I couldn't let that happen. Now, he'll have to go back to the shelter because I'll be in jail."

Bernie knelt next to the young man. "Billie Joe, I understand how important your dog is to you. I get that. I can't keep you from going back to jail, not after trying to burn my barn to the ground. But you can't let the guy who paid you get away with what he was trying to do. If you tell us who it was, maybe we can have some sway with the judge. At the very least, I can ensure your dog is placed in a foster home, not the shelter."

Billie Joe looked up into Bernie's eyes, his own glassy with unshed tears. "You'd do that for me after what I did to you?"

She nodded.

He shook his head. "I didn't kill your goose or poison your dog. I swear to God."

"What about the text with the death threat?" Gerard asked.

"Don't know what you're talking about. Maybe *he* sent it," Billie Joe said. "I don't even own a cell phone."

Bernie met Gerard's gaze.

He turned to Billie Joe. "We'll get to the bottom of that when you tell us who put you up to this?"

"It was that real estate agent, the one with the big black SUV with his name on the side." Billie Joe's eyes narrowed. "Burns. He wanted Ms. Bellamy to sell her place to the big resort trying to move into town."

Bernie had her cell phone out, dialing 911 before Billie Joe finished talking. "This is Bernie Bellamy. Patch me through to the sheriff."

"He'll say I'm lying. No one will believe me over him," Billie Joe said.

She gave Sheriff Bergeron the information, nodded, thanked him and ended the call. "He's got a plan he thinks will smoke out Burns. We have to get you to a hospital first. He said he might get the judge to go easy on you if you agree to let him rig you with a wire."

Gerard nodded. "Burns isn't going to want to leave any loose ends. He'll come to you in the hospital to make sure you don't talk."

Billie Joe blanched. "He'll kill me."

"They'll have you wired and have an officer dressed as a nurse as your backup," Bernie said. "They'll keep you safe. If you want even a slim chance of the judge having mercy on you, you'll do whatever they want you to do to help them get Burns."

"You'll take care of Ruger, my dog?" Billie Joe pleaded.

Bernie nodded. "I promise."

"I'll do it." He reached out and touched her arm. "I'm sorry. You didn't deserve all I did to you. I'm really sorry."

Bernie sighed. "I believe you. You can make it up to me by helping us nail Burns."

"Yes, ma'am."

The sheriff arrived along with an ambulance and two other deputies. While the sheriff and his deputies scoured the area for the shooter, the emergency medical technicians loaded Billie Joe into the ambulance for transport to the nearest hospital.

The sheriff had one of his deputies follow the ambulance to ensure it made it to the hospital without incident. He'd stay with Billie Joe until they could put their plan into place the next morning. Billie Joe's capture would have spread through town by then. Burns would know where they'd taken his henchman.

"We didn't find anyone out there," the sheriff said. "We'll send someone in the daylight to look for the casing. In the meantime, I'll get things set up to bring Burns in."

"It had to be Burns who shot Billie Joe," Bernie said. "He wanted to shut him up."

"But he shot him before he could finish the job of burning down your barn," Gerard said.

Bernie snorted. "Serves him right."

"I'd leave one of my deputies here for the remainder of the night, but I'm shorthanded. If you want, I can stay to make sure the shooter doesn't come back while you sleep."

Bernie shook her head. "Go home to bed. I'm up for the day. It'll be daylight in an hour. I have to be at the farmer's market before sunrise."

The sheriff gave her a gentle smile. "I'm sorry all of this is happening to you. I'll be sure to swing by for some fresh vegetables later in the morning."

Once again, Gerard was touched by how the community looked out for Bernie and her farm.

"Thank you, sheriff," she said.

After all the vehicles left the barnyard, Gerard wrapped an arm around Bernie and led her back to the house. "I'm going to make an omelet. You're going to eat it, and then we're going to drive to town and set up for the market."

She leaned into him. "I'll feel better when they bring Burns in. He could be out there now, ready to shoot again. I don't know why he didn't just shoot me instead of going to all the trouble of trying to ruin me first."

"I'm glad he didn't," Gerard said. "I like to pay my debts, and I still owe you naked cooking." He slapped her ass. "Go get dressed for a great day at the farmer's market. Maybe we'll get word from the sheriff before the day is over, and you can cash in on that raincheck."

"I like the way you think," Bernie said and disappeared into her bedroom.

Gerard was glad they'd caught Billie Joe and that he'd confessed who'd set him up to the trouble he'd caused. But something didn't feel right. Not all the pieces fit. They were missing something.

Billie Joe hadn't mentioned anything about the foot. And what about the ring they'd found in the pigpen?

Where did they fit in this scenario?

He pulled out his cell phone and started to call Remy. His hand paused over the number. It was too early. Why disturb the man's sleep when there wasn't much he could do anyway? He'd bring him up to speed at a more reasonable hour. He could touch base with the sheriff or Hank and Swede and find out if they'd heard anything about the DNA from the foot or the fingerprints they'd lifted from the car in the bayou and the barn's doorhandle.

In the meantime, Gerard had an omelet to make.

CHAPTER 11

With Gerard's help, Bernie had the old produce truck set up, extra tables laid out and a couple of chairs sitting nearby in case business was slow.

The morning flew by. Neither Bernie nor Gerard sat down once.

It was as if the entire town of Bayou Mambaloa had turned out for the farmer's market that day, and everyone made it a point to stop at her truck and buy some of her produce.

Word had circulated that Billie Joe Weems had been captured trying to burn down Bernie's barn. Every customer had to express their concern and delight that they'd caught him, and it was all over. Things could get back to normal at Bellamy Acres.

Bernie smiled and thanked her neighbors and friends, careful not to say anything about Burns, all the while waiting for her cell phone to ring with the news that Burns had shown up at the hospital to silence Billie Joe.

Halfway through the morning, she was shocked when she caught sight of Robert Burns strolling through the market, smiling and laughing as if nothing was wrong.

"Do you see who I see?" Bernie whispered, anger simmering beneath the surface.

Gerard's jaw tightened, the only indication that it bothered him as much as it bothered Bernie to see the man walking around free and clear. "I do."

"I guess the sheriff's plan didn't work," Bernie said. "How can we get him to confess to his part in sabotaging my place?"

"I don't know," Gerard said. "Something's got to give."

Customers converged on the produce truck, and Bernie lost track of Burns. When she looked for him again, there was no sign of the man.

So much for feeling safe. What was to keep him from hiring someone else to do his dirty work? Hell, if he shot Billie Joe and got away with it, what was to keep him from shooting her? That would solve his problems.

With Bernie out of the way, she didn't have anyone who'd inherit the place. What would happen to it?

She hadn't really thought about what would happen upon her death. She hadn't planned on dying anytime soon. Making a mental note to speak to a lawyer on Monday, she continued to smile and sell corn, peas and okra to the generous members of her community.

By two o'clock, many of her bins were empty, and the extra bushels of corn had been sold. She was about to call it a day when her cell phone rang.

Bernie glanced at the caller ID, and her heart immediately started racing.

"This is Bernie," she answered.

Sheriff Bergeron's deep voice filled her ear. "Bernie, we got him."

Bernie's knees buckled, and she would have dropped to the ground if Gerard hadn't chosen that moment to stand beside her.

He slipped an arm around her waist and held her upright.

"Thank God," she breathed into the phone. "We didn't think your plan was working when we saw him here at the farmer's market. I have Gerard with me. Can you tell us what happened?" Bernie punched the speaker button on her phone so Gerard could hear the sheriff.

"He must've made a showing at the market to throw people off. He arrived just after one o'clock when the nurses take turns going to lunch. Our undercover nurse saw him slip into Billie Joe's room. Thankfully, Billie Joe refused painkillers so that he would be coherent when Burns showed up. We got audio evidence of him blaming Billie Joe for botching the job and not finishing it by burning down the barn."

"He said all that?"

"He did," the sheriff said. "When we had enough to book him, our undercover guy moved in just in time to catch Burns holding a pillow over Billie Joe's face."

"Oh my God," Bernie exclaimed. "Is he okay?"

"He's fine and glad they led Burns away in hand-cuffs. He finally got his pain meds and is resting. The judge should be lenient on him after he helped us get Burns' confession."

Bernie sighed. "Thank you, sheriff. I'll sleep better tonight, knowing he's locked up."

"Oh, and Billie Joe had the deputy drop by the room he was renting from Mrs. Crabtree to get his dog. He said you promised to look out for him until he's released."

"I did. The deputy can drop him off at my place in an hour. I'm wrapping up here at the farmer's market and will head that way." Bernie drew in a deep breath and let it out. "Thank you, sheriff."

"No, Bernie," Sheriff Bergeron said, "thank you and that man of yours. If you hadn't been there to catch Billie Joe in the act, Burns would've gotten away with it. Now, he's behind bars for the destruction of property, arson and attempted murder."

As Bernie ended the call, she smiled at Gerard. "My man, huh?" She shook her head. "Thank you for being there to keep me safe and stop Burns from destroying Bellamy Acres." She looked around at the empty bins and baskets. "What do you say we pack it in and head back to the farm?"

"I'm all for it," Gerard said. "Seems like a good night to eat in." His lips tilted in a teasing smile. "I'll cook."

"As long as you're naked," she whispered.

"I can arrange that," he said with a grin.

Happiness bubbled up inside Bernie. She'd just folded one of the chairs when LaShawnda Jones hurried across the gravel in her signature three-inch heels, wearing an eye-popping teal skirt suit and waving her matching acrylic nails. The color complimented her glistening dark skin to perfection.

Bernie envied the woman's ability to always appear dressed like a runway model.

"Bernie, darling," she said as she came to a stop in front of the produce truck. "I'm glad I caught you."

Bernie smiled at her friend. "LaShawnda, I'm sorry, we're just about sold out of everything."

She shook her head. "I just heard about what happened at your place last night and that Robert

Burns was behind it." Her full, luscious lips pursed in a pretty pout. "I'm glad they caught him. He's been impossible to work with since Grand Bijou started buying up property in the area. He was determined to get the bonus they offered to anyone who got you to sell Bellamy Acres to them—that, on top of the commission. I knew he was greedy, but he went too far."

Bernie frowned. "They offered a bonus to get me to sell?"

LaShawnda touched Bernie's arm. "I just wanted you to know I gave them a hard pass. You can't put a price on our friendship. Not even for one hundred thousand dollars." She leaned close and air-kissed Bernie's cheek. "Anyway, I'm glad you're okay, and Bellamy Acres is still yours. Bayou Mambaloa wouldn't be the same without your sweet face here." She turned to Gerard. "Mmm. Aren't you delicious? He's a keeper, Bernie. Gotta go, love. I'll see you later."

As quickly as she swooped in, LaShawnda drifted away, making walking in three-inch stilettos on gravel look like art.

Gerard chuckled. "Who was that?"

"LaShawnda Jones. She's a real estate agent." Bernie's gaze followed her friend, a frown forming on her forehead. "Did you hear that? Grand Bijou offered a hundred-thousand-dollar bonus to whoever could get me to sell."

"No wonder he was so determined." Gerard folded a table, slid it into the back of the truck then piled the chairs on top. "I think we're ready. Do you want me to drive?"

"Yes, please," she said. "I'm getting used to having someone around to help. It'll be a tough transition back to the real world when you move on to your next assignment."

"Trying to get rid of me already?" he said.

"No way. You owe me. I plan on collecting on that raincheck." She leaned back in her seat, a smile spreading across her face. "It'll be nice to be home surrounded by peace and quiet. I love my town and the people in it, but after smiling and greeting folks all day long, I look forward to being alone with you."

As Gerard pulled into the driveway leading up to the farmhouse, he whistled. "I don't think we're going to get the peace and quiet you expected."

Bernie frowned. "What's going on?"

Cars lined the driveway and were parked in the field close to the house. Music blared, and the roar of laughter filtered through the air into the cab of the old truck.

"Someone's having a party," Gerard said.

"At my house? Do you think we're invited?" She recognized some of the vehicles parked in the grass. "Is the entire town here?" Based on the size of the crowd, collecting on that raincheck was again on hold.

Gerard parked as close as he could get to the house. He hurried around to open Bernie's door and helped her down to the grass. "Nothing like being late to your own party," he quipped.

"A party I knew nothing about," she grumbled, disappointed that she wouldn't have Gerard all to herself.

As they approached the throng of people laughing and dancing in the yard, someone shouted, "She's here!"

Everyone turned as one, and a cheer went up that probably reached into the next parish.

Shelby, Felina, Mimi and Gisele converged on her, grinning.

"Were you surprised?" Felina asked.

"Most definitely." Bernie frowned. "But it's not my birthday."

"It's not a birthday party," Shelby said.

Gisele flung her arm wide. "It's a Save Bellamy Acres Fund-raising Carnival."

"Entry to the party is by a donation of your choice," Felina said.

Mimi held out a bushel basket full of money and checks. "The entire town turned out to make sure you don't have to sell Bellamy Acres. We love this place, and most of all, we love you."

"But they bought all my produce today. That was already generous of them."

Mimi laughed. "We bought all your produce so we could have a huge crawfish boil and all the sides. We've been here all day setting up and cooking while you were at the farmer's market."

Bernie shook her head, smiling at the love and generosity of her friends and community. "How did I not know this?"

"The entire town was in on it." Sheriff Bergeron appeared with a roasted corn cob in his hand. "Best corn in the county. I was glad Burns showed up when he did, or we'd have missed the party."

Bernie's eyes widened. "You knew about it, too?"

The sheriff nodded. "Deputy Taylor and her friends dreamed it up after you left yesterday to deliver your melons to New Orleans."

"Word spread so fast we were afraid it would get back to you." Shelby grinned. "Apparently, it didn't."

Gerard slipped an arm around Bernie's waist.

"Did you know about this?" she asked him.

He shook his head. "I've been with you all this time. But I had a feeling they were scheming when we left yesterday. I just didn't know what it was about."

"Come on," Gisele said. "Join the fun." She danced away.

As Bernie and Gerard moved through the crowd,

they came upon Gerard's teammates, drinking beer and playing a yard game, tossing bean bags onto a board with a hole in it.

"Hey, Bernie and Gerard," Remy called out. "Come play a round of cornhole with us."

Gerard held up a hand. "Maybe later."

Remy turned and tossed a bean bag at the far board. It slid up to the hole but didn't go in. "Oh! So close." His cell phone chirped before he could throw another bag. He stepped away from the noise to answer it.

LaShawnda appeared, carrying a can of beer. "Bernie, darling, this man's hand is empty. You gotta keep your man happy, or someone will steal him away." She handed the beer to Gerard. "I might just be the one who steals him away."

"He's not mine to steal, LaShawnda," Bernie said, watching for Gerard's reaction out of the corner of her eye.

LaShawnda practically purred. "You mean, he's fair game?"

Gerard shook his head. "I owe Bernie a date. Until I pay up, I'm not available."

"What kind of date is that?" LaShawnda glanced from Gerard to Bernie and back. She tapped a long, teal acrylic fingernail against her lip. "I think there's more to this date than you're letting on. But LaShawnda doesn't play with her friend's boy toys."

She cocked an eyebrow at Gerard. "Let me know when or if you're available again. I like playing with toys."

"LaShawnda, you hussy, leave Bernie's beau alone," Shelby said.

"He's not my beau," Bernie tried to say, but the music got louder at the point, drowning out her words.

Remy strode back into the group gathered around the cornhole game and walked straight over to Gerard and Bernie, a frown denting his brow. "That was Hank and Swede. They finally got some information about the foot and the fingerprints." He had to shout to be heard over the Zydeco band set up on a portable stage in the middle of the yard.

Bernie's eyes widened. She wanted to hear what he had to say. "Come into the house," she yelled.

Remy, Shelby, Gerard and Bernie entered the house, passing someone on the way out, carrying a six-pack of beer.

Bernie didn't mind. It wasn't like she had anything of value in the house.

Once inside, she closed the door. They could still hear the music, but at least it was muffled by the walls and windows.

"Start all over," Bernie said.

Remy pulled out his cell phone. "Hank and Swede heard from the Louisiana State Crime lab. They found a match on the fingerprints from the car found crashed in the bayou. It belonged to Dean Chauvin, a thirty-eight-year-old man from New Orleans." He held up an image of a man in a mug shot with thick, wavy dark hair, bushy eyebrows and a distinctive nose.

Bernie stared at the image for a long time. The face looked vaguely familiar, but she couldn't quite put her finger on who it reminded her of.

"Chauvin has a rap sheet filled with minor infractions. Nothing life-changing. The problem is the group he hangs with is tagged by Homeland Security and the DEA as New Orleans mafia. He's believed to be the grandson of Vincent Benoit, the New Orleans mafia kingpin."

Bernie shook her head. "And he just happened to crash into Bayou Mambaloa? Why here?"

Shelby frowned. "The deputy who found the car that night said that there were two men with guns near the area where he found the car in the bayou. When he ordered them to put their hands in the air, they fired at him and then took off. They got away in another car. They could've run Chauvin off the road into the bayou and were looking for him when the deputy found them."

"Swede was able to get the DNA info from the crime lab and ran it through a couple of the ancestry databases and found a close match with Vincent Benoit."

"That fits with the fingerprint," Shelby said.

"My grandmother was into the ancestry apps," Bernie said. "I remember coming home from school, and she would be paging through screen after screen on the computer, tracing her family all the way back to Wales. She gave my mother and me DNA tests for Christmas one year."

Remy nodded. "That's what was so interesting about Swede's findings."

Bernie's eyes narrowed. "What else did they learn?"

Remy met and held Bernie's gaze. "Chauvin is a close match to a Bernadette Dupuy."

Bernie pressed a hand to her chest. "My maiden name."

He nodded. "Daughter of Alice and Bernard Dupuy."

Bernie's heart pinched hard in her chest. "My mother and father. I was named after my father, but I didn't have any siblings."

"You and Chauvin could be related as close as half-siblings."

"How old did you say Chauvin was?" Gerard asked.

"Thirty-eight," Remy replied.

Bernie struggled to wrap her head around this.

"Four years older than I am." She held out her hand. "Let me see that photo again?"

Remy held out his cell phone.

"That's why he looks familiar." Bernie left the living room and hurried to the guest bedroom where she'd stored keepsakes her mother and grandparents had treasured. She pulled a wooden box off the closet shelf, opened the lid and shuffled through old photographs of her and her mother. Near the bottom of the box, she found the only photo her mother had kept of the three of them when she'd been a golden-haired toddler.

She laid the box on the guest bed and hurried back into the living room. She held out the photo. "Dean Chauvin is the spitting image of my father at that age."

CHAPTER 12

GERARD LEANED OVER HER SHOULDER, resting a hand against the small of her back. "He has the same hair and facial features as your father. On the other hand, you look like your mother."

Bernie had always been told she resembled her mother. "I think it made it easier for her that I didn't remind her of my father. She never remarried after my father left." She stared at the last picture of them as a happy family of three. "I always hated him for breaking her heart."

"Well," Shelby said, "that's a hell of a note. Kind of puts a damper on our little party here."

"Any idea of why Chauvin was in Bayou Mambaloa?" Bernie asked.

Remy shook his head. "Now that Swede knows he's connected to the mafia, he's putting out feelers to see if anyone is talking about why Chauvin left New Orleans."

Gerard pulled Bernie close. "They'll keep us informed. In the meantime, all of Bayou Mambaloa is here for you."

Shelby nodded. "You might want to say something to them."

Bernie nodded, her head spinning with the knowledge that she'd had an older brother. A sibling she'd never meet if his foot was any indication of what had happened to him. She'd always wished she'd had a brother or sister growing up.

She walked with Gerard out onto the porch and looked over the lawn where people talked, danced and mingled with their friends and neighbors.

These people were her family. They'd joined forces to help her when she'd thought she'd lose the farm.

Shelby strode over to the band. When they finished the song they were playing, she motioned for them to stop.

As an introvert, speaking to crowds had always been difficult for Bernie. When she looked out at the faces looking back at her, she reminded herself they weren't strangers but friends and neighbors she'd known all her life.

She faced them and spoke from her heart. "When I lost my mother, then my grandparents and my husband, I thought I was alone in this world. You have proved me wrong. I'm not alone when I'm surrounded by a community of people I consider family. You're there when I need a hand or just someone to talk to. As I look at all of your faces, I'm overwhelmed with love and joy and thankful I have you in my life. Thank you for your incredible generosity."

As tears slipped from her eyes, someone clapped. Soon, everyone was clapping. As the applause died down, someone shouted. "Let's party!"

The band struck up a lively tune; people laughed, danced and spent time with each other.

Gerard guided her over to where his team had resumed their game of cornhole. While he filled them in on what Swede had discovered, Bernie wandered away, stopping to talk with Remy and Shelby.

Shelby's sister, Chrissy, approached with her husband Alan and their five children.

When Gerard caught up with her, Chrissy's children attacked him.

Bernie's heart swelled at how comfortable he was with them and they were with him.

Gerard dropped to his haunches to give them a great big group hug. As he straightened to his full height, he had the baby on one arm and a toddler on the other. They giggled and hugged his face, pressing wet kisses on his cheek.

Gerard needed to have children of his own. He was patient, playful and gentle with them. The Marine would be a good, protective father despite his fear of turning out like the man who'd raised him.

As sweet as the scene was in front of her, the news that she'd had a brother sat like a heavy weight on her chest, making it difficult for her to breathe.

She drifted to the edge of the crowd, standing quietly while thinking about Dean Chauvin. What had he been like? Did he know his father had another child?

"Ms. Bellamy, dis is quite da party," a deep voice said in her ear.

She spun to face Clayton Fornier, a man who'd been a few grades ahead of her in school. He wore a gray T-shirt that stretched tightly over his barrel chest and thick arms.

Willy Dumas, the man's sidekick, stood on the other side of Clayton. They were always together. Some of the other farmers in the area claimed they'd caught these two men stealing cantaloupe and watermelons from their fields. One farmer said he'd chased them out of his cornfield one night. If they'd taken any of her produce, Bernie wasn't aware and gave them the benefit of the doubt. "Clayton, how's your sweet mother?" she asked.

"She's all right, I guess," he answered.

"Willy, I hear your little sister is getting married

soon. Is she here tonight?" Bernie looked around at the crowd.

"No, ma'am. Izzy spends most of her time in Baton Rouge with her fiancé."

Clayton moved closer and lowered his voice. "We figure you found what was out in your field da other night."

Bernie tensed. Her first thought was of Dean Chauvin's foot. She nodded slowly, wondering how much these two men knew about the disappearance of her half-brother. "What do you know about it?" Though her gaze was on the band, she kept watch on the two men in her peripheral vision.

"Just dat we ain't da only ones lookin' for it," Willy said. "Da others are more dangerous."

Bernie frowned, not sure they were talking about the same thing but afraid she'd spook them if she asked outright what the hell they were talking about. "What do you suggest I do with it?"

"If you give it to us, dey won't have no reason to come after you," Clayton said. He nodded to the crowd of people. "You got all you need."

"Ah, there you are." Gerard joined her and slipped an arm around her waist. "Friends of yours?" he asked, nodding toward the two men.

"Clayton Fornier and Willy Dumas, this is Gerard Guidry..." she paused and added, "my bodyguard."

The two men stiffened, their eyes widening.

"Nice to meetcha, Mr. Guidry," Clayton said. "Willy and I were jest leaving."

"We are?" Willy looked confused.

"Yes, sir." Clayton nodded to Bernie. "Let us know what you decide." He grabbed Willie's arm and hurried away from Bernie and Gerard.

"Bodyguard, huh?" Gerard cocked an eyebrow.

Bernie's lips twisted. "That was the strangest conversation."

"You didn't look comfortable. Do I need to flex my bodyguard muscles with them?" Gerard puffed out his chest and flexed his arms.

Bernie laughed. "All you had to do was look at them, and they ran off." She shook her head. "I think they might know something about the foot we found."

"Oh, now, I definitely need to flex my bodyguard muscles and get them to talk."

She told him what the two had said. It made no more sense when she repeated it than when she'd heard it the first time.

"We should let the sheriff know to question the pair," Gerard said.

"I think he left a little while ago," Bernie said. "We can let him know in the morning. I doubt Clayton and Willy will leave town suddenly."

The band switched from a lively tune to a slow, sultry one.

Bernie leaned into Gerard. "I don't suppose you like to dance?"

"If, by dance, you mean standing in one place and swaying, then yes, I like to dance. Would you like to dance with me?" he asked.

"I thought you'd never ask." Bernie turned into his arms, pressing her body against his, wishing all the people would go away so that she could be alone with Gerard on what might be their last night together.

The thought depressed her.

When the song ended, Bernie excused herself, claiming she needed a trip to the bathroom.

She entered her house and found her way to the bathroom, the quietest place around. When she shut the door, she could barely hear the music.

For a long moment, she stood absorbing the silence. She'd needed some alone time. As a farmer, she spent most of her days working outdoors, alone. Though she loved her neighbors and friends, being around people all day was exhausting.

She splashed water on her face and dried off, knowing she couldn't hide there forever.

Taking a deep breath, she left the bathroom and her bedroom. As she passed the guest bedroom, she noticed the wooden box she'd left on the bed. She entered the room, gathered the loose photographs, placed them back in the box and closed the lid.

Her mother had treasured the ornate box and the

items she'd saved inside, including the photo of their little family. Though she'd struggled to support Bernie by herself, her mother had never said a bad word about Bernie's father.

When she turned toward the closet with the box in her hands, she tripped over something on the floor, lost her balance and crashed to the floor.

The box she'd been holding hit the wall, the bottom breaking loose from the sides. A single envelope skittered across the floor and came to rest near Bernie's hand.

Bernie sat up and pulled the box across her lap. When she reached for the bottom piece, she realized it wasn't broken but knocked loose. She slid it back into the box, and the panel blended perfectly; it was a secret compartment.

The envelope that had drifted out must have been secreted into the hidden compartment.

Bernie lifted the yellowed paper and read the handwriting on the front.

My Love

Intrigued, she opened the envelope and pulled out a single sheet of paper written in bold, masculine strokes.

My dearest Ali,

My past mistakes have caught up with me and threaten you and my sweet Bernie's very existence. I would never forgive myself if anything happened to my girls. You are my everything.

Alas, a brief affair I had before I met you resulted in a son I knew nothing about until today. His mother, the daughter of a very dangerous man, is dying of cancer and demands that I raise her son within her family. When I told her I couldn't, she threatened to have you and Bernie killed. Her family does not know about you two and won't know as long as I stay with our son and raise him in her family.

The only way to keep you and Bernie safe is to do as she asks. It means leaving the two people I love the most forever. If I try to contact you, they will know. I thought of running away with you both, but I'm being watched all the time. These people are ruthless and wouldn't hesitate to kill a woman and child. I can't let that happen. I love you too much.

So, I'm leaving. You will not hear from me. I will not contact you. Know that you and Bernie will be forever in my heart.

With all my love,
Bernard

TEARS STREAMED DOWN Bernie's cheeks as she read the last words her father had written to her mother so long ago.

He hadn't abandoned her because he didn't love

them. He'd left and hadn't contacted them to keep them safe from the woman's family.

Part of Bernie wanted to hold onto her anger at having been abandoned. Her father could have tried harder. He should have found a way to spirit them away to a safe location where they would have remained the happy little family they'd been.

But from what she'd learned about her half-brother, he belonged to a mafia family. It could be one of those families that, once you joined it, you couldn't leave unless they carried you out in a box. Or threw you in a river with cement overshoes.

What had brought Dean to Bayou Mambaloa? Had their father sent him? Was her father still alive?

Bernie gathered the box and the letter and pushed to her feet, eager to find Gerard and show him the letter that proved her father hadn't left because he didn't love them, but because he loved them. When she turned toward the bedroom door, she froze.

A man dressed all in black, wearing a ski mask, pointed a gun at her.

"Where is it?" he demanded.

"Where is what?" she asked, her voice trembling.

"You damn well know what," he barked.

A surge of anger pushed through her veins. "No, I damn well don't. If it's the foot you want, you'll have to go to the state crime lab to get it."

"I'm not after a goddamn foot," he growled. "I want the bag," he said.

"What bag?" she shot back.

"The bag he stole. I know you have it."

"What's with you men thinking I have something that I don't?" She set the box on the bed to free her hands in case she had to fight for her life. "Who stole what bag? And what's so special about a bag?"

"Your half-brother, Dean, stole a bag filled with three-hundred-thousand dollars in cash." The man in the mask's eyes narrowed. "The family wants it back."

"The family or you?" Bernie asked. She was stalling, hoping someone—Gerard—would notice she'd been gone too long and come find her. "If the family was that concerned about the money, wouldn't they have sent more people to retrieve it?"

"They sent me," he said.

"Or were you in charge of safeguarding the money, and Dean absconded with it on your watch?" She laughed. "That's it, isn't it? You have to get that money back, or they'll come after you, thinking you stole it."

"Shut the fuck up," he said. "Give me the goddamn money."

She crossed her arms over her chest. "I don't have it."

"Then get it," he commanded.

The man wasn't going to believe she didn't have

the money. The problem was that he had a gun. There were a lot of people in her yard and going in and out of her house. If this man started shooting, the innocent lives of her friends would be lost.

She had to do something to disarm this man without getting shot or getting other people shot in the process.

"It's not in this room. I hid it in the barn," she lied. If she could get him out of the house and into the barn, she'd have more room to work on getting that gun out of his hand. Holy shit. She'd never had to disarm a gunman.

Before she'd married Ray, she'd never driven a tractor, milked a cow or stuck her arm inside a pregnant cow's hoo-hah to help it birth its calf. She'd done a lot of things she'd never done before. How hard could it be to disarm a gunman?

Gerard, where are you? This damsel is in distress and in need of a knight in shining armor to save her ass.

CHAPTER 13

BERNIE HAD BEEN GONE LONG ENOUGH to use the bathroom, take a shower and bake a cake.

Gerard was heading for the house to find her when Bayou Mambaloa's Laurel and Hardy ran up to him, breathing hard, their eyes wide as if they'd seen a ghost.

"Bodyguard dude," the one called Clayton said in a rush. "Where's your girl?"

"Where's Bernie?" Willie demanded.

"Why?" Gerard stalled. "What's wrong?"

"It's not good. Not good at all," Clayton said.

"Lost ten years off my life, I did," Willy exclaimed.

"Slow down," Gerard said, "and tell me what's got you so freaked out."

"It's only da second dead body I've seen," Willy muttered. "I don't like it. It ain't right."

"What dead body?" Gerard asked.

"The one behind the barn," Clayton said.

Gerard wanted to check on Bernie, but the two men were so freaked out, he had to see this dead body first. "Show me," he said.

Clayton and Willy led the way around to the back of the barn. Gerard rested a hand on the pistol tucked into his waistband. He'd be ready if these guys were trying to pull one over on him.

"There," Clayton stopped and stepped aside, pointing at a body lying on the ground, dressed all in black and wearing a black ski mask. "That's one of the two guys." He looked round nervously.

"Question is, where's da other?" Willy said.

"We told Ms. Bellamy to give us the bag," Clayton said. "We'd take it off her hands, and they wouldn't come after her."

The two men weren't making sense. Gerard had reached his limit of nonsense and wanted to get back to Bernie. "What bag?"

"Da one we took off da dead guy before we tossed him in with da pigs," Willy blurted out.

"Willy!" Clayton punched his friend in the arm.

"What?" Willy rubbed his arm. "We didn't kill him, just disposed of his body and that damned goose." Willy shrugged. "*You* killed the goose."

"Damned thing attacked me. It was pure self-defense."

Gerard held up a hand. "Let me get this straight. You took a bag off a dead guy, threw him in with the pigs and killed Bernie's goose?"

"It attacked me," Clayton insisted.

"What was in the bag?" Gerard asked. Before either man could answer, Gerard's cell phone rang. The caller ID indicated it was Swede. He answered.

"The New Orleans Mafia is wound up tighter than a top over a bag of missing money to the tune of three-hundred-thousand dollars."

Gerard glanced at the two men in front of him as he repeated the amount out loud, "Three hundred thousand dollars?"

"Yeah. Three of their men are missing. Chauvin and two others. The entire mob is looking for them with orders to bring back that money no matter how many people they have to kill."

"We can account for two of the three. There's still one outstanding." Gerard was already on the move before he ended the call.

Clayton and Willy hurried to catch up. "What about the dead dude?" Clayton asked.

"Call 911," Gerard called out over his shoulder.

The band still played. People laughed and danced, oblivious to the danger they could face.

Gerard didn't have time to warn anyone. He had to get to Bernie before the other mafia man did.

It all made sense now. The foot, the text message

Bernie had received warning her to give back what she had or die. She'd thought it was the realtor, trying to scare her into selling her property.

Instead, it was the mafia wanting their money back.

He bet it had been the mafia guys who'd poisoned Howey to keep him quiet while they'd searched the barn.

Since the last mafia guy standing of the three hadn't found the bag of money, he would be convinced Bernie had found it and hidden it somewhere they wouldn't find it.

But she didn't have it. And neither did the men who'd taken it from the dead guy.

They needed to find it before anyone else got hurt.

Gerard raced up the steps onto the porch and entered the ranch house. As he crossed the living room toward the bedrooms, the guest bedroom door swung open.

Bernie stepped out, her body stiff and her chin held high.

"Bernie!" Gerard rushed forward.

"Gerard, don't," she commanded.

He skidded to a stop, his heart sinking like a lead weight in his belly when she moved enough to the side that he could see behind her. A man dressed in black with a black ski mask held a gun to Bernie's temple.

"Oh, babe," he said.

She gave him a weak smile. "I'm showing him where the money is hidden in the barn."

Gerard knew the money wasn't hidden in the barn and that Bernie had only told the lie to buy some time.

"My finger is resting on the trigger," the masked man said. "Make a move toward us, and I'll shoot her."

"It's okay," Bernie said. "I'll give him the bag, he'll be on his way and this will all be just a bad dream to forget."

An idea sprang into Gerard's head. "The bag from the barn?"

Bernie nodded, her brow knitting ever so slightly.

"You remember I moved that bag from the barn back to the house." He bent to retrieve the bag he'd packed with all his clothes, hoping it was close to the same size and color as the bag of money this terrorist expected.

The man holding the gun at Bernie's head lifted his chin. "Toss it here."

"Okay, on three," Gerard pointed two fingers down so that Bernie's captor couldn't see what he was doing.

Bernie gave an almost imperceptible nod.

Gerard gripped the bag in both hands.

"One," he said and tensed.

"Two."

Gerard launched the bag straight at Bernie.

At the last second, she ducked.

The bag hit the gunman full in his masked face.

The gun went off, Bernie dove for the floor and Gerard threw himself after the bag, knocking the gunman to the ground. His gun flew from his grip and landed several feet away from the man.

Bernie scrambled on all fours, grabbed the gun and pointed it at the man in the mask.

Shelby erupted into the room, her gun drawn, followed by the Brotherhood Protectors, ready to protect and defend.

Gerard straddled the piece of shit who'd tried to kill Bernie. He wanted to slam his fist into the man's face for even pointing the gun at his woman.

Shelby pulled a zip-tie out of her back pocket and secured the man's wrists behind his back.

Gerard left the guy on the ground and pulled Bernie into his arms. "I just lost a couple dozen years off my life."

"I thought you'd never get here," she said.

"I was busy. Your friends Clayton and Willy found this guy's partner behind your barn."

"Dead?" she asked.

He nodded. "Shot."

"All for a bag of cash," Bernie said. "You know this problem isn't going to go away until the money is located, don't you?"

"Two men have died for that bag of cash," Shelby said. "It might not even be here anymore."

"Clayton and Willy confessed that they took it off your brother's body and stuffed it into the base of a hollow tree. When they came back for it, it was gone."

Bernie shook her head. "Who else would have known it landed here?"

"Word gets out," Shelby said as she led her prisoner through the living room. "It might be a good idea to disperse the crowd. If the mafia gets wind the bag ended up in Bayou Mambaloa and traces it to Bellamy Acres, it could get ugly."

"Leave the money where they can find it, and they'll go away," the prisoner said.

"How about we leave you where they can find you?" Shelby said.

He shrugged. "My days are numbered. They probably already think I stole it and killed the other two so that I could keep it all to myself."

"Well, you'll be safe in a jail cell for a very long time for the murder of your partner," Shelby said.

The man snorted. "There's nowhere safe from them. I won't last a week, even in a maximum-security prison."

Shelby snorted. "Guess you should've thought of that before you got involved with them." She tossed her car keys to Remy. "Could you have someone bring my cruiser up to the front of the house?"

Remy nodded and handed the keys to Lucas, who immediately left the house to follow orders.

Bernie looked up into Gerard's eyes. "I don't want anyone else hurt because of that money."

He nodded and dropped his arms from around her to take her hand in his. "Let's thank everyone and tell them you'd like to call it a night."

She nodded. "I'd rather be a party pooper than have anyone hurt."

"It might be better if they don't know about the danger," Remy said. "There won't be a mad rush to get out of here."

Bernie's hand tightened in his as they stepped out onto the front porch.

"Hey, Bernie," a voice called out. "We have another surprise for you." Mimi waved a hand toward a man walking up the road from where all the cars were parked.

As he neared, Gerard could make out the man's features. It was the veterinarian, and he had a large hound dog on a leash.

As they neared, Bernie cried, "Howey!"

The vet bent, unclipped the leash from the dog's collar and let him go.

Howey, in his gangly lope, his ears flopping, raced toward the house.

Bernie bent down and called out, "Come on, Howey. Come to Mama."

The dog didn't slow until he reached the porch steps.

Instead of climbing up to Bernie, he darted to the right and disappeared beneath the porch.

Bernie laughed. "He's probably disturbed by all the people." She descended the stairs and crouched low to peer beneath the porch. "Howey? Come out, sweet boy."

The dog whined but remained where he was.

Gerard pulled out his cell phone and turned on the flashlight, then squatted beside Bernie.

When he shined the light beneath the porch, it reflected red off the hound dog's eyes.

"Come on, boy. Come to Mama," Bernie coaxed.

In the beam of light, Gerard noticed a variety of items scattered beneath the porch. "I see what you mean by Howey's treasures."

Bernie laughed. "I really need to get under here and clean it out. It's been a while. Come on, Howey. I want you to stay in the house tonight."

"I'll get him," Gerard said and dropped to his hands and knees.

"Please, don't," Bernie said. "It's too dirty, and there are spiders and maybe even snakes."

"I don't want Howey staying out all night, either," he said and handed her his cell phone. "Hold the light."

She aimed the light at an angle toward the dog so that Gerard could pick his way through the items the dog had collected.

When he reached Howey, he scratched the dog behind his ear and spoke softly. "It's okay, boy. We just don't want anyone to hurt you. Come on." He snagged the dog's collar and started to drag him out. As the dog moved, Gerard could see what appeared to be a gym bag beneath him.

What were the chances?

He hooked his fingers through the handle and crab-crawled backward, dragging the dog and the bag. As he came out from under the porch, Howey ran for Bernie.

She wrapped her arms around him and hugged him until he squirmed.

Gerard stared down at the bag in his hand, his heart pounding as he slid the zipper open.

"What have you got there, Gerard?" Remy leaned over his back. "I'll be damned."

Gerard turned to Bernie, a smile spreading across his face.

"What is it?" she asked.

"Howey had the bag of money all along," he said.

Her brow furrowed. "You're kidding." Holding

onto Howey's collar, she moved closer. "Holy cow. It's probably been there since the first night."

Gerard zipped the bag before curious party-goers gathered around.

At that moment, Lucas arrived, easing Shelby's cruiser through the crowd and stopping in front of the house.

Shelby came out the front door with her prisoner and escorted him to the cruiser, tucking him into the back seat.

She joined Gerard and Bernie beside the porch. "What's going on?"

Gerard shoved the bag full of money toward Shelby. "We found the money. It needs to go into evidence ASAP. And, by all means, leak it to the news. The mafia needs to know the money has been recovered and turned over to the state police."

Shelby took the bag. "Got it."

Remy slipped an arm around her. "We'll make sure it gets into the right hands." He turned to the other members of the Brotherhood Protectors. "Valentin, Landry, Jacque, Sin. You'll be our escort."

The men gathered around Shelby as she climbed into her cruiser. Remy got into the passenger seat.

Shelby drove slowly through their neighbors and friends, with the four men walking alongside her. Once they reached their vehicles, they loaded up. One truck moved in front of Shelby, the others fell in behind her. Moments later, three vehicles drove toward the gate.

They slowed as another sheriff's vehicle with lights flashing entered Bellamy Acres, followed by an ambulance.

By that time, the band had stopped playing and had begun to pack up their equipment. The party-goers gathered their blankets, chairs and children, an air of confusion mixed with concern heavy in the air.

Gerard climbed the steps to the porch and called for their attention. "Bernie appreciates everything you all have done for her, and she hopes you've had some good food and a good time here at Bellamy Acres. Thank you for coming. Right now, there are some matters that need to be cleared up with law enforcement. Rest assured, you're all safe, and Bernie is safe. Members of the Brotherhood Protectors will help direct traffic leaving the farm. Please drive carefully, preferably with a designated, sober driver."

Bernie took Howey into the house to feed him and get him settled.

Gerard met with the sheriff, bringing Clayton and Willy along to explain their part in the drama and the disposal of Chauvin's body.

The emergency medical team zipped the dead mafia guy into a body bag and loaded him into the back of the ambulance.

It was nearing midnight when the last vehicle departed, leaving Gerard alone with Bernie.

They stood on the deck, looking out at the debris left behind from the party.

"It can wait until tomorrow," Gerard said.

"Tomorrow." She smiled sadly. "It's all over, isn't it?"

He nodded. "Now that the money has been recovered, the mafia won't have a reason to come after you. You'll be safe."

She nodded. "I'll move on with my life, and you'll move on to your next assignment."

"You know, you haven't cashed in that raincheck I owe you," he said.

She shook her head. "You don't owe me anything. I owe you my life. Not only did you save me, you reminded me that life isn't all about work. It's about relationships, community...and love. I've pushed all of that aside over the past three years. It's time I started living again."

He nodded, his chest tightening. This felt like goodbye, and it hurt more than being shot or hit with shrapnel.

He'd always walked away, never looking back. Never thinking about who the woman was sleeping with after he left. One time, he'd run into a woman he'd dated a couple of years before. She'd been pushing a baby stroller with a beautiful baby girl all dressed in pink ruffles.

He hadn't been the least jealous. In fact, he'd congratulated her on her marriage and baby, truly happy for her.

He tried to imagine his reaction if he encountered the same scenario, only the woman was Bernie with a baby that wasn't his.

His chest burned with something he'd never felt before. He pressed his hand against the spot with no relief.

Bernie with a baby.

She'd make a great mother. Kind, caring, protective. What if she married a man who turned out to be like Gerard's father?

Gerard wouldn't be there to protect her and her baby.

The thought made his fingers clench into fists.

"I told you from the start, no commitment, no regrets." Bernie turned to face him. "Only I lied. To you. To me." She laid her hands on his chest and met his gaze with a fierce one of her own. "I committed my heart in our first kiss. I had no choice. It's what my heart wanted. When you walk away like you promised you would, I'll wonder if I did enough to make you stay. I'll regret not trying harder. So, here's me, trying harder." She leaned up and pressed her lips to his. "We've only just met, but we've lived a lifetime in the past forty-eight hours. I know in my heart you're the one for me, and, damn it, I'm the one for you."

Gerard's heart swelled to the point he thought it might burst from his chest.

Tears welled and spilled down her cheeks.

Her tears gutted him.

He reached up to brush them away and bent to touch his lips to hers.

"What if I turn out to be like my father?" he whispered.

She smoothed her fingers along his cheek. "What if you don't? We only live once, and we don't even know how long that might be. I won't pass on a chance for happiness. Either one of us could've died tonight. Would you have died with regrets? I would have. I would've regretted that I didn't tell you how I feel, that I didn't kiss you enough or make you realize what an incredible man you are." She curled her fingers into his T-shirt and yanked him closer. "Don't leave," she said, her eyes flashing with her passion.

"I can't," he said, a sense of release welling inside.

She continued. "Don't walk away from a life filled with happiness, children and love."

"I won't," he said, brushing a strand of her hair behind her ear.

"You're kind, gentle with children and in complete control of your emotions. You'll never be like your father. You're better than him and worthy of all the happiness your heart desires."

Gerard's lips spread into a grin. She was so caught up in convincing him to stay she hadn't heard him.

She stared into his face, her cheeks blooming with color. "You have to understand what an incredible—"

Gerard covered her mouth with his, stemming her flow of words. As the kiss deepened, she melted against him.

When he lifted his head, he smiled down into her eyes. "We've only known each other a couple days—"

"The heart knows what the heart knows," she countered.

"Shh." He pressed a finger to her lips. "Let me finish."

She nodded, kissed his finger and let him continue.

"You say I saved you when, in truth, you saved me. I shut people out when they got too close. But you didn't let me. You showed me what I didn't realize. I can be kind to children. I can control my anger." He brushed a kiss across her forehead. "I can love without hurting the ones I love."

Bernie wrapped her arms around him. "You deserve to love and be loved," she said. "You're a good man. And if I'm not the one for you, there's someone out there who is. You just have to open your heart."

"Bernadette," he said, liking the way her full name sounded. "My heart is open. To you."

She looked up into his eyes. "You mean that? You're not saying that because you feel sorry for me, and my begging got to you?"

He laughed. "I mean it. The thought of walking away from you nearly brings me to my knees. I can't do it. I want to be with you. I want to get to know you better. I want..." he swallowed hard, "I want to have babies with you."

She laughed, the sound catching on a sob. "You're not afraid?"

"Sweetheart, I'm terrified." He crushed her to his chest, burying his face in her hair. "But I'm more terrified of losing you. Of wasting time second-guessing my ability to be a good father. I want you. I want a life with you. A family filled with children, love and laughter. I think I've always wanted it but was afraid I could never have it."

She raised his hand to her cheek, tears streaming down her face. "We can have all of that. Together."

EPILOGUE

Gerard stood at the stove in the farmhouse he now shared with Bernie, making scrambled eggs while coffee brewed on the counter behind him.

He wore nice slacks, a white button-down shirt and patent leather shoes. It had been a long time since he'd worn a suit. Thankfully, Bernie had helped him pick out this one. She'd assured him he could use it for multiple occasions, including their wedding, just three short months away.

He'd wanted to get married sooner, but Bernie's friends talked her into waiting long enough for them to secure a venue and schedule all the things women expected at a wedding.

Bernie said none of that mattered to her, but it made her friends happy to be involved, and she was happy her friends were happy. So, she'd agreed to go along for the ride.

Wearing the suit today wasn't for a happy occasion but more for closure.

After learning Dean Chauvin was her half-brother, Swede looked further, searching for Bernie's father. He found him listed as Bernard Chauvin, former resident of New Orleans. He'd died over a decade before —the cause of death: heart failure. Bernie had visited his grave in New Orleans and seemed to have made peace with the memory of her father.

A week ago, the state crime lab had released Dean Chauvin's foot into Bernie's custody. No one else stepped forward to claim it. Not even his kingpin grandfather. Bernie arranged for the cremation and wanted to conduct her own small service for the half-brother she'd never known.

"I didn't know him, and he might not have been a good person," she'd argued, "but at one point in time, he was someone's baby. He deserves a send-off."

Thus, the suit and the patent leather shoes that were still too stiff to be comfortable.

They'd collect the urn from the mortuary and drive over to a point on the bayou where Bernie's father had taken her fishing as a little girl. They'd say a few words, release Dean's ashes and be home in time for lunch.

"Uh, Gerard?" Bernie's muffled voice called out from somewhere in the master bedroom or bathroom.

"Yes, dear?" he responded.

"Remember that night I collected on the naked cooking raincheck?" Her voice was moving closer.

Gerard smiled. They'd cooked lasagna, and he'd made love to her on the kitchen table, on the counter and against the wall. "I remember."

"Remember how we only had the one condom but made love three times?"

He chuckled. They'd searched the house for more but hadn't found any and had made love anyway.

Bernie appeared in the doorway, wearing only a bra and lacy panties.

God, she was sexy. His groin tightened. Grease popped in the pan, and he returned his attention to the eggs he was about to burn. "I remember."

Her voice softened. "Remember how we said we'd wait until after we were married to remodel the guest bedroom and start trying to have children?"

His head shot up, and his gaze locked with Bernie's.

She brought her hand up from behind her back and waved a plastic wand. "We might want to rethink our project timeline."

Gerard's heart leaped in his chest. He let out a *whoop!* Across the floor in seconds, he crushed her in his arms. "How? When? Is it a boy or a girl? What will we name him? Holy shit! I better get that room remodeled."

Bernie laughed. "We have time. Eight months should be enough to get ready for baby Guidry, between your work, my farming and the wedding."

"Babe." He shook his head, his heart so full he couldn't come up with words that expressed his happiness. "I love you."

Bernie smiled, her face glowing. "I love you. And this is just the start. I want at least four children. We'd better plan an addition to the farmhouse in the very near future."

"I'll make it happen." He grinned. "We're going to have a baby."

"We're going to have a house fire if you don't turn off the stove."

Gerard started over with fresh eggs like he'd started over life when he'd found Bernie. It was up to him to do it right. With Bernie, he had the confidence and courage to be the best person he could be.

For Bernie and, now, for their baby.

LUCAS

AYOU BROTHERHOOD PROTECTORS
BOOK #3

New York Times & USA Today
Bestselling Author

ELLE JAMES

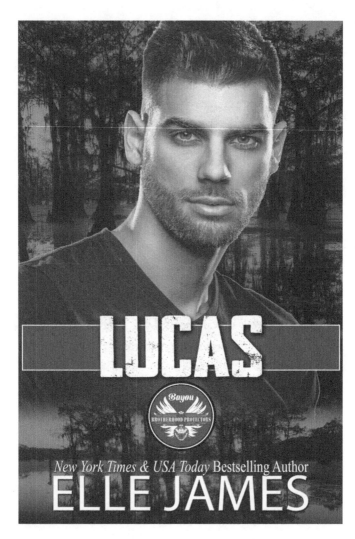

LUCAS

New York Times & USA Today Bestselling Author

ELLE JAMES

CHAPTER 1

"DANNY, we're gonna need more beer over here," Bernadette "Bernie" Bellamy waved at their friend and favorite waitress at the Crawdad Hole Bar and Grill.

Felina Faivre slid lower in her chair, her cheeks burning. "I haven't finished the beer I have. It's not that big a deal. Really."

Too late. Danielle French, the feisty little red-haired dynamo everyone referred to as Danny, hurried over and rested her empty serving tray on one hip and her fist on the other. "Who is he? What's he done? Do I need to stomp on his hairy ass to get his attention?"

Bernie nodded. "I'm all for it, but Felina has decided to take the high road."

Danny frowned. "Who are we talking about? New

guy or Marty the rat bastard who dumped you for your best friend?"

"Shh." Bernie pressed a finger to her lip. "Marty asked Trish to marry him," she whispered.

Danny's eyes widened. "Has it even been two weeks since he dumped you?"

Felina grabbed Danny's arm. "Please. It's not that big a deal."

"The hell it isn't," Danny said, her voice growing louder. "No one treats our favorite flower girl like gator excrement and gets away without some form of retribution."

Felina grimaced. "I appreciate your loyalty, but I'm really okay. We were drifting apart anyway. I should've seen it coming, but I was too busy with my shop to pay attention to our relationship."

"Meanwhile, he was screwing your best friend," Bernie pointed out. "For him to pop the question to Trish, they had to be going at it for longer than you two have been broken up."

"No shit, Sherlock," Danny said. "Want me to get Gisele to conjure up a Voodoo potion to give the jerk a massive case of jock itch?"

"Did I hear my name?" Gisele Gautier, the granddaughter of the local Voodoo Queen, sailed up to the table and slid into the seat on the other side of Bernie. She grinned. "Who are we plotting against? I love brewing up a little retribution."

"No, guys." Felina shook her head. "I don't need vengeance. I need ideas on how to make it through the wedding without looking pathetic."

"What wedding?" Gisele asked.

"Marty asked Trish to marry him," Bernie filled Gisele in.

Gisele let out a low whistle. "Seriously? So soon?"

Felina's gut twisted at the reminder. She and Marty had been a couple since high school. Everyone in Bayou Mambaloa had expected them to get married, even Felina. She'd thought he was waiting to propose until he'd established himself as a successful insurance agent and she'd gotten her flower shop business solvent enough to hire another person to help. They'd both met their career goals, and he'd still not asked her to marry him.

Felina felt like she'd somehow failed at their relationship. She'd failed to see the truth. Marty hadn't asked her to marry him because of career timing. He hadn't wanted to marry her, period.

Gisele reached across the table and covered Felina's hand. "Do you want me to turn Marty into a frog?"

Felina gave a shaky laugh. "No, I don't." She squeezed her friend's hand. "I'm actually happy for Marty and Trish and wish them all the luck."

Danny snorted. "Trish will need all the luck. If he

could dump you for her, who's to say he won't do that to Trish?"

"I can't think that way," Felina said. "Trish is my best friend."

Gisele's eyes widened. "Still?"

Danny frowned. "She stole your man. How can you still call her a friend?"

"She didn't steal him," Felina said.

"Did I hear you say someone stole something?" a feminine voice sounded behind Felina.

She turned to smile weakly at Shelby Taylor. "Nothing important."

"Only her boyfriend's heart," Danny said.

"Are you off duty tonight?" Felina asked, trying to steer the conversation away from her problem.

Deputy Shelby Taylor wore jeans and a white blouse instead of her uniform. "I'm on days this week. I'm meeting Remy here for dinner." She pulled up a chair and dropped onto it. "What did I miss?"

Felina closed her eyes, knowing the others would bring Shelby up to date on her dilemma.

"Trish stole Marty from Felina," Danny said.

"And now, they're getting married," Gisele added.

"She didn't steal him from me," Felina argued. "Apparently, I never owned his heart. He fell in love with Trish. I can't fault him for that. She's beautiful and nice."

"And duplicitous and not your friend if she was

having an affair with Marty behind your back." Gisele's lips pressed together.

"You're too kind," Shelby said. "I'd dump her ass."

Felina shook her head. "I can't. I'm the only florist in Bayou Mambaloa."

All four women stared at her as if she'd lost her mind.

"Please, don't tell us you're going to do the flowers for their wedding," Danny said, shaking her head.

Felina grimaced. "I promised Trish I would."

"Forget the beer," Bernie said. "Bring the whiskey."

Danny marched to the bar, reached over the counter, grabbed a bottle of whiskey and four glasses, plunked them on her tray and hurried back, calling over her shoulder, "I'm taking my break. Don't bother me for fifteen minutes."

"Ladies," Felina said. "I don't want this to get blown out of proportion. I'm really okay with all of it."

"Obviously, you're not, or you wouldn't be at the Crawdad Hole on a Thursday night." Danny unscrewed the cap from the whiskey bottle and filled the five glasses. She handed one to Felina while Shelby, Bernie and Gisele snagged a glass for themselves. Danny sank into the seat beside Felina. "Here's to friends who don't screw your boyfriend."

"Hear! Hear!" Bernie, Shelby and Gisele chorused.

Felina's lips twisted. "I'll drink, but only because I know the whiskey's good. And, to be honest, I do need help."

"And you came to the right place." Danny drank her glass of whiskey in one long gulp, then plunked the glass on the table. "So, what's it to be? Want me to put a hit out on Marty? I know a couple of coonasses who'd do it for a bottle of whiskey."

Shelby pressed her hands to her ears. "I did not just hear that."

"No," Felina said. "I just want ideas on..." she fought for the right words, "frankly, how to save face and get my mother off my back."

Bernie blinked. "Sweetie, you don't need to save face."

"She's right," Gisele agreed. "If anyone needs to save face, it's Trish and Marty."

"You know Bayou Mambaloa," Felina continued. "Everyone is feeling sorry for me. I'll be the biggest, most pathetic loser at Trish's wedding. If I had dumped Marty, it would be different. He dumped me; therefore, I'm the loser."

Gisele shook her head. "Felina, you have it all wrong. You're the winner. Marty didn't deserve you."

"She's right," Shelby said. "You dodged a major bullet."

"I know that," Felina said. "But my mother and the rest of our little gossipy town are feeling sorry for me. I don't want that. I need a plan to look strong, not weak."

"Then why did you agree to do the flowers for their wedding?" Gisele demanded.

"Yeah," Danny said. "You should've told them to shove it where the sun won't shine."

How did she get through to her well-meaning friends that she didn't want to come off as mad or vindictive? "I want to appear to be happy for them. But not in a pathetic way."

Shelby tapped her fingernail against the tabletop. "They need to think you've moved on to something better."

Bernie touched a finger to her chin. "You need to look like you dumped Marty for a better option." Her lips twitched and then stretched across her face. "You need a hunky wedding date."

Felina frowned. "I have to live in this town. How's that going to help when he only appears for the wedding and disappears afterward? I'll look like I can't keep a man."

Danny's eyes narrowed. "You could have your wedding date appear a couple of weeks before the wedding for the buildup."

"Then you could stage a breakup at the wedding. Only, you do the breaking up this time," Bernie offered.

"He'd have to be much better looking than Marty," Gisele noted.

"Absolutely," Bernie said.

"Nothing else will do," Shelby agreed.

Danny nodded. "And you have to have a go-to-hell dress that makes Marty regret dumping you."

"That's not necessary—" Felina started.

"Hell yes, it is," all four of her friends said at once.

Felina laughed. "Assuming I go along with this plan, where am I supposed to find a better-looking guy than Marty? He's one of the best-looking guys Bayou Mambaloa has to offer."

"True. Bayou Mambaloa doesn't have much to offer in the way of native men," Gisele said. "Besides, you need someone bulked up and maybe a little more dangerous looking."

As if conjured from Gisele's words, the door to the Crawdad Hole Bar and Grill opened, and ten men entered.

Each guy had broad shoulders and muscular arms. They looked like they could chew nails and spit them into boards.

"What about them?" Danny said.

Bernie grinned. "No kidding. Any one of them would be perfect, except my Gerard."

"And my Remy," Shelby added, raising a hand to her fiancé, Remy Montagne. "For that matter, you could hire one of them. Granted, the Brotherhood

Protectors are more in the line of security or protective services than paid dates. They're all former special operations operatives with years of experience on the battlefield."

"Yeah, but could they handle the small-town battleground and the minefield of a wedding?" Gisele asked.

Bernie frowned. "Maybe some more than others. Wouldn't hurt to ask."

"I don't know..." Felina eyed the men, considering her friends' words. She wouldn't look so pathetic if she had one of these hunky men at her side for the next couple of weeks and as her date to the wedding.

Marty couldn't hold a candle to their flames. Especially the tall one with dark hair and bedroom eyes. She'd seen him around town. He'd even been into her shop on several occasions to purchase small vases of flowers. Probably for his girlfriend. Which meant he was completely out of the selection pool. He'd introduced himself as Lucas.

At that moment, Lucas looked her way and smiled.

Felina's heart fluttered, and a swarm of butterflies erupted in her belly. Holy hell. The man went from smoldering good looks to panty-melting-hottie with one stretch of his lips.

"It's a solid idea worth checking into," Shelby said as she pushed to her feet. "Do you want me to put a bug in Remy's ear and find out if someone would be willing to take the job?"

Heat filled Felina's cheeks. "No," she said quickly before Remy reached Shelby. "I want to think about it."

"Hey, beautiful." Remy stopped in front of Shelby, pulled her into his arms and kissed her soundly. When he finally raised his head, he smiled down at her. "Miss me?"

"Mmm. A little. Remind me again why." She lifted her chin, and Remy kissed her again.

Felina's heart swelled for her friend. As a friend and a deputy sheriff, Shelby did so much for the people of Bayou Mambaloa. She deserved to be happy. And Remy made her happier than Felina could remember Shelby ever being.

What they had, the love they shared, was how it should be. Not the boring existence she'd had with Marty. She was glad he'd dumped her. It had saved her the trouble. However, since he'd left her, she'd been stopped on the street where neighbors and townspeople expressed their condolences and openly pitied her.

Some of her customers came to the shop just to tell her how sad they were that Marty had dumped her after all this time, leaving her unmarried and with no chance of finding a husband at her advanced age of thirty. If she waited too long, her eggs would dry up, and she'd never have children.

Her own mother was already setting her up with any unmarried man she could scrape up, determined to get a grandchild before she died. After all, Felina wasn't getting any younger.

"Guys," Danny said. "Get a room."

Shelby and Remy broke apart.

"Not a bad idea," Shelby said. "Do we have any food at home?"

"I think there's one slice of pizza left in the refrigerator," Remy said.

Shelby sighed. "It's enough for me, but you need more." She glanced at Felina. "Are you sure you don't want me to say anything?"

Felina's cheeks heated. "I'll figure out something."

Shelby shrugged. "I'm sure they could help."

God, she hated to think about all ten of the men knowing what a failure she was that she had to hire a date for a wedding. Maybe she'd take one of her mother's offerings. As soon as the thought surfaced, she squashed it. *Not in a million years.*

Why settle for weeds when you could have a bouquet of muscles?

No. She'd come up with some other way of deterring the gossips and appeasing her mother. Maybe she'd plan a vacation after the wedding, like an unhoneymoon to celebrate her near-miss.

Shelby and Remy moved toward a table where several of his friends had gathered.

Bernie stepped into Gerard Guidry's arms and tipped up her chin to receive his kiss. "Hey."

Felina swallowed hard on a groan. "I have to go."

"But you just got here," Danny said.

"And we haven't picked out your guy," Gisele added.

"I'm not convinced it's a good idea, and I need some air." Felina tipped her head toward Bernie and Gerard.

"Oh." Danny's lips pressed together. "I get it. Misery loves company, not a reminder that some people are ecstatically happy." She rose from her chair. "I have to get back to work anyway. Do you want me to walk you out to your car?"

"No, I'll be fine. It's still early," Felina said.

"Never too early for the drunks to get stupid," Danny said with an arched brow.

"I've got my pepper spray." Felina pulled the small container from her purse.

"Yeah, well, keep your hand on it," Danny said.

"I will." Felina headed for the rear door.

The man called Lucas appeared in front of her. "You're not leaving, are you?"

Felina's heart skipped several beats. She shook her head. "No," she lied. "I need to visit the ladies' room."

"Oh, well, don't let me hold you up." He stepped to the side. "When you get back, I'd like to buy you a drink."

Felina scurried away, wondering if Shelby had spilled the beans to this hunkworthy man that her pathetic friend needed a man in her life—at least for a wedding she didn't want to attend.

Holy hell. Would the humiliation never cease?

She headed for the hallway leading toward the rear exit, passing the bathrooms on the way. She didn't slow until she pushed through the door into the balmy night air.

For a moment, she stood on the back landing, breathing deeply until her heartbeats slowed and she could think straight.

She was about to step off the landing when the back door slammed open, and she turned halfway around to see who it was.

A man rushed through so fast that he plowed into Felina, nearly knocking her off the stoop.

He wrapped his arms around her to keep them both from flying off the landing. "What the fuck," he muttered, teetering on the edge.

Headlights flashed at one end of the gravel parking lot.

The man's hand slid into her front jeans pocket.

"Don't touch me!" Felina demanded as she positioned her little can of pepper spray over her shoulder, hoping to get the man's eyes and not hers. She pressed the button.

The man yelled and pushed her so hard she flew off the stoop, landing on her hands and knees in the gravel, the pepper spray skidding out of reach.

She looked back at the man above her.

"Fuck!" The man swayed on the stoop, rubbing his eyes.

One more step in the wrong direction and he'd fall, landing on top of Felina.

He took that step.

Felina tucked and rolled back toward the stoop as the man tumbled off the landing.

He landed in a heap on the gravel in the spot she'd just vacated.

He staggered to his feet, his eyes tightly closed. "Bitch! I'm gonna kill you!"

Before Felina could rise to her feet and run, a black SUV with darkly tinted windows blew through the back alley and skidded to a stop in front of the man she'd pepper-sprayed.

A big man, wearing a dark suit and sunglasses, leaped out of the SUV, grabbed the man by the shoulders, shoved him into the back seat and climbed in beside him. The door slammed, and the SUV spun out of the parking lot.

Felina lay in the shadow of the stoop, waiting for the SUV to move far enough away to allow her to read the numbers and letters on the license plate. Unfortunately, there was no license plate.

The SUV disappeared around the corner of the building.

Felina pushed to her feet and stared down at her bloody hands and torn jeans.

The back door opened, and a man stepped out.

Felina tensed, ready to run.

The man's face was cast in shadow from the light shining down on the back of his head.

When he turned toward her, he murmured. "What the hell?"

Felina whirled to run. Before she could take two steps, the man flew off the stoop, landing in the gravel beside her.

He grabbed her arms and spun her around.

"Let go of me!" she yelled and pounded her fists against his chest.

"Felina, it's me, Lucas," he said in a low, rich tone. "It's okay. It's just me."

She stared up into the warm brown eyes of the man who'd bought multiple bouquets of flowers in her shop. When her mind registered him as a friend rather than an enemy, she sagged against him.

"Sweetheart," he said softly, "are you hurt?"

"Not much," she whispered.

He tipped her chin up and stared down into her eyes. "What the hell happened?"

ABOUT THE AUTHOR

ELLE JAMES also writing as MYLA JACKSON is a *New York Times* and *USA Today* Bestselling author of books including cowboys, intrigues and paranormal adventures that keep her readers on the edges of their seats. When she's not at her computer, she's traveling, snow skiing, boating, or riding her ATV, dreaming up new stories. Learn more about Elle James at www.ellejames.com

Website | Facebook | Twitter | GoodReads | Newsletter | BookBub | Amazon

Or visit her alter ego Myla Jackson at mylajackson.com
Website | Facebook | Twitter | Newsletter

Follow Me!
www.ellejames.com
ellejamesauthor@gmail.com

ALSO BY ELLE JAMES

Gerard (#2)

Lucas (#3)

Beau (#4)

Rafael (#5)

Valentin (#6)

Landry (#7)

Simon (#8)

Maurice (#9)

Jacques (#10)

Brotherhood Protectors Yellowstone

Saving Kyla (#1)

Saving Chelsea (#2)

Saving Amanda (#3)

Saving Liliana (#4)

Saving Breely (#5)

Saving Savvie (#6)

Saving Jenna (#7)

Saving Peyton (#8)

Saving Londyn (#9)

Brotherhood Protectors Colorado

SEAL Salvation (#1)

Rocky Mountain Rescue (#2)

SEAL Justice (#13)

Ranger Creed (#14)

Delta Force Rescue (#15)

Dog Days of Christmas (#16)

Montana Rescue (#17)

Montana Ranger Returns (#18)

Brotherhood Protectors Boxed Set 1

Brotherhood Protectors Boxed Set 2

Brotherhood Protectors Boxed Set 3

Brotherhood Protectors Boxed Set 4

Brotherhood Protectors Boxed Set 5

Brotherhood Protectors Boxed Set 6

Iron Horse Legacy

Soldier's Duty (#1)

Ranger's Baby (#2)

Marine's Promise (#3)

SEAL's Vow (#4)

Warrior's Resolve (#5)

Drake (#6)

Grimm (#7)

Murdock (#8)

Utah (#9)

Judge (#10)

The Billionaire Daddy Test (#4)

The Billionaire Matchmaker Test (#5)

The Billionaire Glitch Date (#6)

The Billionaire Perfect Date (#7)

The Billionaire Replacement Date (#8)

The Billionaire Wedding Date (#9)

Cajun Magic Mystery Series

Voodoo on the Bayou (#1)

Voodoo for Two (#2)

Deja Voodoo (#3)

Cajun Magic Mysteries Books 1-3

The Outriders

Homicide at Whiskey Gulch (#1)

Hideout at Whiskey Gulch (#2)

Held Hostage at Whiskey Gulch (#3)

Setup at Whiskey Gulch (#4)

Missing Witness at Whiskey Gulch (#5)

Cowboy Justice at Whiskey Gulch (#6)

Boys Behaving Badly Anthologies

Rogues (#1)

Blue Collar (#2)

Pirates (#3)

Made in United States
Cleveland, OH
21 December 2024

12501628R10157